SOMEWHERE
IN THE
HOUSE

Also by Elizabeth Daly
in Thorndike Large Print

The House Without the Door
Nothing Can Rescue Me
Unexpected Night

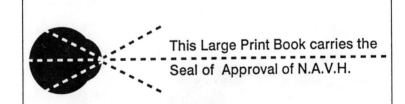

This Large Print Book carries the
Seal of Approval of N.A.V.H.

SOMEWHERE
IN THE
HOUSE

Elizabeth Daly

Thorndike Press • Thorndike, Maine

Library of Congress Cataloging in Publication Data:

Daly, Elizabeth, 1878-
  Somewhere in the house / Elizabeth Daly.
    p. cm.
  ISBN 1-56054-323-X (alk. paper : lg. print)
  1. Large type books. I. Title.
[PS3507.A467S6   1992]   92-4316
813'.52—dc20   CIP

Thorndike Press Large Print edition published in 1992
by arrangement with Henry Holt and Company, Inc.

Cover design by Carol Pringle.

The tree indicium is a trademark of Thorndike Press.

This book is printed on acid-free, high opacity paper. ∞

Contents

I

THE WINDOW

The voice on the telephone was deep for a woman's, sad and slow. It asked: "Is this really Mr. Gamadge himself talking?"

"This is Gamadge."

"I'm Harriet Leeder — Mrs. Clayborn Leeder. It's such a private matter that I shouldn't have liked to give anybody else my name. Might I ask you not to mention the fact that I called to anybody at all, whether you are able to help me or not?"

"I won't mention it."

"You don't know me, but friends of yours do. I haven't told them anything — only that I needed advice. It's a family thing, and rather horrid. From what they say, I really think you may be my only hope."

Gamadge had not been giving his full attention to the speaker. He stood at the telephone table in the hall, looking through the double doorway of the library; and the scene he watched was nerve-racking. His young assistant, David Malcolm, stood in the middle of the room with an arm upraised above his head, and on his palm the Gamadge baby was balanced as a waiter balances a tray. The baby, mildly interested as usual, made swimming motions with its arms and legs.

Gamadge said loudly: "Put that thing down before you break it."

"I beg your pardon?" asked the telephone.

"I beg yours." Gamadge waited until the baby had been lowered to the rug, and then apologized again: "I'm awfully sorry. I was interrupted."

"We can't be overheard?"

"Absolutely not."

"I know I shouldn't be taking a moment of your time, much less asking you to come to see me. Our friends say that you're just back from Europe, and that you were hurt there."

"Nothing much," mumbled Gamadge. "I just got in the way."

"Intelligence?"

"Not at that precise moment," said Gamadge, laughing. "Counter-Intelligence, as a matter of fact."

"It's shocking of me to ask you to leave your family, even for an hour. An hour this afternoon, and then if you felt you could agree to take the job on — not a nice job at all — it would mean an hour or two tomorrow."

"No more than that?"

"You'll think it quite enough, I'm afraid."

No friends of Gamadge's were likely to refer anybody to him without good cause. He said: "If it's very urgent —"

"You may not think so. Could you possibly come up and hear about it? Come at four, for tea? Perhaps you know our old brick house; the Clayborn house."

A vision of red brick and tiled gables rose before Gamadge's inner eye. He said: "Of course I know the Clayborn house, Mrs. Leeder," and wondered what that name was trying to say to him. Clayborn. Leeder. There was something.

She went on: "Just off the Park. I really have no one to turn to. If you decide to be charitable, you could stay on and meet the family at five. We all live here, as you may know, and if we're in town we all meet for tea at five. I should like to be able to tell them that *you* will represent me."

"Represent you?"

"My interests."

"I have no standing of any kind, Mrs. Leeder, that would qualify me to —"

"I'll explain. Will you come? Or does it all sound too strange? I can't say more over the telephone."

Gamadge looked at his watch, and then gazed mournfully across to the library. He said: "Strangeness is a recommendation to me, you know."

"I was depending on that." The sad voice quickened. "I *may* expect you at four?"

Clayborn? Leeder? The names certainly had a meaning for Gamadge, but what was it? He was sure it wasn't an agreeable one. He said: "I'll be there."

"You don't know how grateful I am. In half an hour?"

"Half an hour."

Gamadge put down the telephone. Annoyed at having so little time for research, and at being prevented from asking questions of his wife, he opened the telephone book. He found *Clayborn, Gavan,* and the address — not much more than a mile up town. Lovely day, he would walk.

He got the Social Register off its shelf. His client was there, and it looked as though she were divorced; she was down as Mrs. Harriet Clayborn Leeder. No Mr. Leeder seemed to be anywhere.

Under *Clayborn* there was quite a list — Gavan, Miss Cynthia, Seward, Garth, Miss Elena (who was still at college). He began to remember something of the family now — a family better known in the nineteenth century than it was to-day. It had been going strong in the '70s, '80s and '90s; in New

10

York society, in diplomacy, in high sporting circles — he was sure that there had been a Clayborn racing yacht.

One or two elder Clayborns had tried literature; there had been reminiscences of European embassies, there had been a book of travels and big-game hunting. And not so long ago a Mrs. Clayborn, Gamadge was certain, had been a patron of chamber music.

They were not so much in the news nowadays. Gavan Clayborn, to judge by his clubs, still took an interest in yachting. Seward, a non-sporting character, went in for first-class clubs whose members more or less followed the arts. Garth Clayborn, named for the sporting and writing ancestor, had only achieved one of the family clubs as yet — an athletic institution of great fame. He must be young. Last of all came Miss Elena Clayborn, still at college. No clubs, poor child, at all.

Gamadge went into the library. His wife Clara was reading beside a window, his assistant David Malcolm was standing the cat Martin on its hind legs, and the baby, very masculine in shorts and a little sweater, was watching them affably from the rug.

Gamadge said: "I have to go out."

Clara moaned. "Henry, why will you an-

11

swer the telephone and get caught in this way?"

"Because my alleged assistant never answers it."

"I never can remember to," Malcolm said. "Damn."

"That's going to be the baby's first word," said Clara.

"Look here," said Malcolm. "It's the nurse's Saturday afternoon off. Suppose I push the pram?"

"You stick to your job," said Gamadge. "Learn something about books. All you know now is that if a book's cover is coming off it isn't worth as much as it would be if its cover wasn't coming off."

"But you can't go out," said Clara. "David's Miss Lucas is coming to tea, and we were going to have a rubber of bridge. When will you be back?"

Gamadge said angrily that he didn't know, and strode from the room.

Clara looked after him. "He didn't tell us anything," she said. "That means it's a case. He isn't fit; his arm's very stiff yet. This is horrible."

"If it's a case," remarked Malcolm, "why didn't he ring me in on it? That's what I'm supposed to be for."

"It must be a secret one," said Clara, "and

I hate them. Call up somebody, Dave; we can't disappoint Miss Lucas." She added: "Too much."

"My moral responsibility towards Miss Lucas," replied Malcolm, "is nil."

"Just make that clear to her then, will you?" Clara's expression was stern. "Because I'm not at all sure that she knows it."

"Make it clear to her? How?" asked Malcolm, perplexed. "I can't very well assume that she assumes what you assume she does, can I?"

"Oh, bother!" said Clara. "Just talk to her the way you talk to me."

"That I can't do," protested Malcolm, "because there isn't anybody else like you."

"There," said Clara. "That's what I mean."

"But that," replied Malcolm, in hurt surprise, "is conversation."

Gamadge, meanwhile, with his stick in his hand and a light overcoat on his arm, was walking west towards Park Avenue. It was a bright and beautiful October day in 1944, with a briskness in the air that would turn to a chill later, and his doctor had formally requested him not to catch cold.

"You're too old and you've been too sick to pretend that you're immune to the weather," Hamish had told him.

So Gamadge had the top-coat over his arm.

Thirty-nine years old and medium tall, with a slight stoop and a long, lurching stride, he was a figure in monochrome; rather colourless as to hair and skin, and with greenish-grey eyes. Quite unself-conscious, he would have been astonished to hear that there was something about him which caught the eye.

He turned up Park Avenue, and suiting his pace to the time allowed him, arrived at the Clayborn street just before four o'clock. He walked to Madison and then towards Fifth, where the Park trees were now a blur of yellow-green, with bare branches already stark among the dying leaves.

The east gable of the Clayborn house, three storeys high, rose above the tiled roof of its old two-storey carriage house and stables. These had been turned into studio apartments with skylights, the original double doors remaining to accommodate tenants' cars. The house itself, like its outbuildings, was of dark-red brick, brick as expertly chosen as the tiles and the pinkish stone of the trim. When the front elevation came in sight Gamadge paused to admire it; it must be, he thought, an H. H. Richardson; few examples of his art, so solid and yet so decorative, now remained in New York, and most of those were stables — converted as the Clayborn stables had been.

Yes, it was typically Richardson — the bands of windows below, the tall, triple-arched windows under the gables. Gamadge retraced his steps to look up at the east gable again, and its triple window. This window was false — or had it been bricked up? The bricks within the delicate stone framework seemed lighter and newer than the rest.

Gamadge walked on to the ornamental arch that led into a deeply recessed porch or vestibule; walked past it, past the house, and along a high brick wall that enclosed a garden; trees showed above the stone coping. There was a narrow alley between the garden wall and the next house, and Gamadge, looking through to the street beyond, saw that a gate in the Clayborn wall gave on the alley.

He returned. The house had no basement, the rough stone foundations rose from grass, and the low bands of the first-floor windows were head-high from the ground.

He went up two shallow steps and into the porch; rang, and was admitted by a very old butler who smiled at him.

"Mr. Gamadge?"

Gamadge said yes, smiled in return, and gave up his hat, coat, and stick.

"Mrs. Leeder would like you to come upstairs, Sir."

As they crossed the large, dark, oak-beamed

15

hall, Gamadge reflected that the only thing against these houses was their darkness. They were always dark, and how their architects had loved dark oak, stone fireplaces with andirons as tall as Great Danes, tapestries, bronze wall-torches, Chinese pots as big as wash-tubs, chairs to accommodate Henry the Eighth himself. They were all here, all the trappings; including tapestries with velvet borders and a vast oriental rug.

Gamadge was half-way up the stairs behind his guide when he paused — with one foot in the air. He remembered at last who Mrs. Leeder's husband had been. He put the foot down and continued the ascent; his mind ranging back to dim memories of a great scandal and a celebrated case. Rowe Leeder had been mixed up in the case until an alibi got him off. At that time he had been married only two years, to Miss Harriet Clayborn.

What was the case? The murder of a show-girl, or ex-showgirl, named Sillerman. Gamadge remembered no details, he had been still at his university; it had happened twenty years before. All he could recall were loud reverberations — Leeder had been a well-known figure about town, the only son of an excellent family.

The house was as silent as the grave. Gamadge and the old butler were mounting as quietly as ghosts to the thickly carpeted landing. Gamadge had to remind himself that such houses were always quiet ones, built and furnished for quiet. Absurd to suppose that the Clayborns could still be effacing themselves, overshadowed by that old scandal. Leeder long ago had been cast out of their lives.

He followed the butler across a wide hall and through an arched doorway into a big room that extended all the way to the west end of the house. A dark room, lighted by low windows, but a handsome and a comfortable one. Big old-fashioned floor-lamps stood beside armchairs flanked by low tables, dark oils in tarnished gilt frames broke the wall space; there was one, a portrait of a high-nosed old gentleman of the seventies, above the mantel.

The butler said: "Mrs. Leeder will be here in a moment, Sir," and went away.

Henry Gamadge stood looking about him. Windows on either side of the fireplace, in which a wood fire burned; windows to the west, darkened by the apartment building across the alley-way. Cushioned seats below them, matching the red brocade of curtains and upholstery. At each end of the hearth a sofa at right angles, and in this little enclosure, in front of the left-hand sofa, a large round tea

17

table furnished with a tremendous tea service and tray in repoussé silver. Behind this sofa rose a great three-leaved Chinese screen to cut off draughts from the window beyond it.

Gamadge turned as Mrs. Leeder came into the room, her hand held out to him. She was a very tall, slender, dark and handsome woman in her forties, with a white skin; she had a look of settled melancholy. She wore a long dress, the skirt black and the bodice of shimmering purple. Antique silver and diamond ear-rings were brilliant below her black hair. She said: "I know how good this is of you, Mr. Gamadge. Please don't ask me who urged me to beg this favour of you."

"Are you afraid I'd reproach them?" He smiled. "I wouldn't."

"I hope they'll forget all about it and never ask me whether I did call you."

"Perhaps they'll ask *me*."

"No, they won't do that." She turned to lead the way across the room, then stopped. "Will you have a cup of tea with me, or shall Roberts bring you something more fortifying?"

"I'd like tea very much."

She went on, but instead of going directly to her place at the tea tray she glanced first behind the screen. When she faced him again she showed embarrassment. "So silly of me," she said, "but I can't break myself of doing that. Will you sit opposite me and make yourself comfortable on that sofa?"

They sat down, Gamadge at the end of the sofa, where he had a small table beside him.

"When my cousin Garth was a little boy," she explained, pouring hot water into the teapot, "he used to hide behind that screen and listen to conversations. Since he's twenty-five years old, or will be tomorrow, he's probably outgrown the habit. But I still look behind the screen."

"A mild obsession," said Gamadge, "unless you're not really sure that he has broken himself of the habit."

"Perhaps I'm not sure that people ever really change. They may seem to, but . . ." She emptied the tea-pot, put tea into it, and poured on boiling water. She sat back. "He's supposed to be out for the afternoon with Elena, and the others won't turn up until five at the earliest." She paused and looked at Gamadge: "Sugar? Lemon? Cream?"

"Just sugar, please. One spoonful."

She poured out his tea. Roberts came in with cakes and sandwiches, saw that Gamadge was supplied, left the plates on a stand beside the table, and handed Gamadge his cup. Then he retired.

"He won't come back until I ring," said Mrs. Leeder, "and *he* won't listen. He knows all our secrets, and he loves us all. What was I saying? Oh — about the plans of the family for this afternoon. Uncle Gavan plays bridge at his club on Saturday; afterwards he's going to pick Aunt Cynthia up — she's at the first Clayborn Quartette concert of the season. Did you know that Grandmother founded the Quartette?"

"I knew she did a lot for string music in New York."

"None of us cares much for it any more, but Aunt Cynthia thinks one of us ought to go to the concerts. I'm afraid art is dying out among the Clayborns, though Seward still does some designing; but he resigned from the firm in 1934. Graff Textiles."

"Beautiful work they turned out."

"He really ought to have been an artist, but he's never been quite strong. He rests in the afternoons until Roberts calls him for tea, and that" — she gave him her dim smile — "accounts for Seward. Elena is his only child, and I suppose I ought to explain that Garth was the only child of another Clayborn, now dead. Both his parents died when he was a baby, and he was installed here then."

Gamadge felt in his pockets; she said: "Won't you try one of our cigarettes?"

"Thank you, I'll stick to mine. But let me —" Gamadge followed her glance, which was directed towards the little table at his elbow. It was crowded with objects, including his cup of tea, but he saw no cigarette box there.

Mrs. Leeder smiled again. "You're looking at one of Seward's and my masterpieces. He has a splendid studio and work-room on the top floor, and he used to have lots of hobbies. So did I, before I was married."

A book, nicely bound in old morocco, lay on the little table. Gamadge picked it up, opened it, and found it no longer a book; its pages had been glued together and neatly hollowed out into a box. It held cigarettes.

"You made this? A nice job," he said, offering it to her. "I like these things."

She took a cigarette, and Gamadge lighted it for her. Then, after lighting one of his own, he turned the box in his hands.

"We made lots of them," said Mrs. Leeder, "out of old books of Grandfather's that the family said we could use. The house is full of solanders, and we gave them to people for Christmas."

"Solanders? Well . . . a solander really means a box made to look like a book; perhaps it's in order to use the term for a book made to look like a box."

"You have a passion for accuracy, Mr.

21

Gamadge, haven't you?"

"People complain of it."

"I don't."

Gamadge looked at the gold letters on the faded crimson spine. He read aloud: *Journals of Sir Arthur Wilson Cribb in the Punjaub,* 1861.

"Uncle Gavan seemed to think that we shouldn't be vandals," said Mrs. Leeder, "if we made a solander out of that book."

"Well, of course Cribb wasn't Sleeman or Sherwood, Shakespeare or Meadows Taylor," said Gamadge, "but I'm not at all sure that I should have made a box out of his journals in the Punjaub."

"No? Why not? Do you mean you actually know the book?"

"I'm slightly acquainted with it, or was."

"Oh dear, what have we done? Was he important? Was he an army man?"

"Civil servant. But we won't," said Gamadge, laughing, "waste time on him this afternoon; or on Thagi, the Sacrifice of Sugar, and the Consecration of the Pickaxe."

"What on earth?" Her dark eyes questioned his in pleased wonderment. "You do know everything, don't you? They said you did."

"They frightfully exaggerate, whoever they are."

"But I'm so glad you do. You're quite right,

Mr. Gamadge — we must put off the Sacrifice of Sugar till another, happier time. Now I must tell you why I asked you to come. I said that tomorrow will be Garth's twenty-fifth birthday. That's the day set in my grandmother's will for winding up a trust. The estate will be divided up amongst her heirs, and we can sell the house; and on Monday an agent's coming to view it. So tomorrow we must open a door."

II

THE DOOR

"Open a door?" Gamadge looked at her, his cigarette half-way to his mouth. And as she said nothing, he asked: "Do you mean the door of a safe, Mrs. Leeder? I hope my friends didn't tell you I could do that! I don't even know an obliging cracksman!"

"It isn't a safe; it's a room." She added as if reluctantly: "It's been shut for twenty years."

Gamadge, watching her downcast face, offered a short monologue: "I hate them too — attics full of family relics. Some delight in them; to me they represent stuffiness, and they're full of gadgets you can't guess the use of. And moulting stuffed birds are grisly; so are creased garments and pressed flowers."

"I wish it were an attic. It's just a room that's been sealed since my grandmother died."

"By her orders?"

"No; we sealed it. Now it must be opened

24

and cleared out, and all the heirs must be here when it's done — my uncle Gavan, my aunt Cynthia, Seward and Garth, and my former husband Rowe Leeder. He's one of the heirs. I want you to be here too — at three o'clock tomorrow afternoon."

"Why?"

"That's what I find so hard to tell you; but I must, and if I do some explaining first it won't be so difficult for me or seem so queer to you. First I ought to explain that Rowe Leeder comes here quite often. Grandmother never cut him out of her will after that terrible thing that happened to him — that Sillerman scandal; perhaps you've heard of it?"

"I remember something."

"She only lived for a week or two after it, she died of a stroke; but I think she wouldn't have cut him out of the will anyway. She was very fond of him. None of us, of course, ever thought for one moment that he had anything to do with the girl's death, and he was completely exonerated — he had an alibi." She was playing with a little silver trident for spearing slices of lemon; and Gamadge noticed that she still wore a wedding ring. She went on after a pause: "But his name got out through some bungling, and it was in the headlines. My father and mother made me divorce him. If I'd been older — but I was only twenty-four. I let them persuade me."

Her voice died away. Presently she went on: "After they died, he drifted back. As an occasional caller, you know. It seemed to happen quite naturally. I was very glad. And the family —"

She laid down the silver trident and looked at him. "I hope you won't be too shocked at my attitude towards them. They're very cynical; they don't mind what people do — only the scandal. It had died down by the time Rowe came back, and they accepted him quite coolly. As an heir — we all share equally — he had a certain standing; you'll understand why when I tell you about the will.

"And I can't tell you about it without telling you first about Grandmother — and Nonie."

"Nonie?"

"She's dead. She was Grandmother's youngest child, and she died ever so long ago, in 1914, just before the other war. There were six children: Uncle Gavan, Aunt Cynthia, Seward's father, my father, Garth's grandfather, and Nonie. They're all dead but Uncle Gavan and Aunt Cynthia, and so are their wives. So the estate is to be divided among us — Uncle Gavan, Aunt Cynthia, Seward, Rowe Leeder, Garth and me. Elena wasn't born until after Grandmother died; she doesn't come into it at all except through her father.

"Grandmother had all the money, you know; she brought it into the family. By that time there wasn't much left among the Clayborns — they never made money themselves, they married it and they spent it. Grandmother was quite used to being surrounded by fortune hunters, she rather liked them. They're always attractive, naturally, and she could manage them.

"She managed everything, and after Grandfather died she simply ruled the house. Her last will was made in 1922, just after I married, to include Rowe Leeder. He amused her, they got on, and he had only his salary in the bond-selling business.

"Now, of course, there won't be so much to go around as she thought there would be. We'll all have enough to live on, but we shall need every penny.

"I ought to explain that the estate has been in trust until now, and the house kept up from a fund paid us annually by the executors; the sole executor now is the bank. One of the agents appointed in Grandmother's will to administer the fund and all our allowances is Mr. Allsop, who was Grandmother's lawyer — so was his father; that firm has been the Clayborn lawyers for generations.

"We've all lived on those allowances ever since Grandmother died, and we couldn't possibly have lived anywhere else on them. We're allowed vacations," said Mrs. Leeder, with her dim smile, "but we must live here — until tomorrow, when the trust is wound up and the estate is divided among all the heirs. If we had tried to break the will the money would all have reverted automatically to that wretched Clayborn Quartette."

Gamadge said: "These restrictive clauses in wills are very trying, I might almost say iniquitous."

"You don't quite know how restrictive the clauses were. Nothing in the house was to be changed or removed, nothing done at all unless in the way of necessary repairs, and Mr. Allsop had to be consulted about those. You must understand that he isn't concerned with *our* interests — all he's concerned with is carrying out the provisions of the will. We never dared to try to break it — we never risked it. So here we are" — she looked vaguely about her — "and here we have been since November, 1924."

"Your grandmother must have had a tremendous feeling about the house."

"Oh, it wasn't that. It was all on account of Nonie."

"You said she died thirty years ago."

"But not for Grandmother. She was the apple of her eye. The rest of us are assertive

28

in our different ways, all the Clayborns were; all but Nonie, who wasn't except by birth a Clayborn at all. She was a phantom, or rather she was clay in Grandmother's hands. From her infancy she had a little white room next to Grandmother's, and Grandmother chose her clothes and her amusements, her friends and her books. She never went out alone; she was a delicate little thing, I believe. It was all shocking and not quite wholesome. She was Grandmother's obsession, and had no life of her own.

"Except for her music. She had some talent for the piano, and Grandmother took it seriously. Not that Nonie would ever have been allowed to play professionally, of course, but she had the most expensive masters. And when Grandfather — who was the only person with any influence over Grandmother at all — when he complained of the eternal practising, Grandmother had a room at the top of the house sound-proofed at huge expense."

Gamadge asked suddenly: "Did the sound-proofing include bricking up a window?"

Mrs. Leeder smiled a little. "Not much escapes you, Mr. Gamadge."

"I happened to notice the paler bricks in it."

"It wasn't bricked up until afterwards. Well, Nonie died, in the spring before the other war, and at first they thought Grand-mother would lose her mind, or die too.

"She shut herself into her rooms for weeks, she wouldn't see anybody but her companion, a sort of distant relative, Aggie Fitch. This Fitch woman was the most awful little syco-phant. She lived here, and she encouraged Grandmother in all her whims, and helped to spoil Nonie. I got most of these details from my elders, of course — principally from my mother. I was only fourteen when Nonie died, and at school and keeping early hours. I can just remember my Aunt Nonie: a wraith. A pretty blonde wraith, with Grandmother's colouring — the Clayborns are apt to be big and dark-haired and strong. She was always exquisitely dressed, and she was as spoiled as any other pet.

"We ought to have realized that Grand-mother *hadn't* collapsed after Nonie's death; that she was incapable of collapse. We soon found out what she had been secretly doing with Aggie Fitch's help. But I sometimes wonder —" Mrs. Leeder picked up the tiny silver trident from the lemon tray again, and impaled a slice of lemon on it. She looked at the slice, and then replaced it. "We all some-times wondered whether Grandmother hadn't gone a little off her head after all. But she was never insane in the medical or legal sense

30

— oh, never! We have had plenty of opinions about that. You'd be surprised, Mr. Gamadge, to find out what peculiar things you could do and remain sane in the eyes of the law.

"While she was shut up in her rooms, in what we thought a stupor of grief, she had been very busy; she had been turning Nonie into a fetish. Grandfather was dead by that time, of course — he wouldn't have allowed it for a moment. I can see a Clayborn allowing it! Any Clayborn with authority, I mean. There were plenty of protests."

Gamadge asked: "A fetish?"

"She had got hold, through the Fitch woman, of an artist in wax."

"Oh."

"Really an artist. He had photographs and measurements to work on, a coloured portrait, Nonie's white dress and shoes, and her hair."

Gamadge, looking rather daunted, gazed fixedly at Mrs. Leeder.

"We didn't even know," she continued, "that Grandmother had had the hair cut off before Nonie was in her coffin. Well, the masterpiece came home and was fastened invisibly to the piano stool in the sound-proof music room, with its hands spread out on the keys. Nonie's treasures — her principal ones — were put there with her, and Grandmother used to sit and worship there."

31

"Good Heavens."

"Delightful thing to live with, wasn't it? And the door being locked when Grandmother wasn't there — that made it worse. I only had a glimpse or two of the thing — I used to run past the room when I went up to the studio — and I used to dream that it came to life."

"Naturally."

"No servants were allowed into the room to clean it; Grandmother and Aggie Fitch kept it spotless. You can see how convenient the sound-proofing turned out to be; sound couldn't get out, moths and dust and mice couldn't get in."

"A sealed box."

"Almost; it is a sealed box now. Well; Grandmother knew how we hated the whole thing, and how we dreaded the possibility of the story getting out and into the papers. It never did; the old servants were loyal, they knew that they were all provided for in Grandmother's will. And Grandmother herself didn't want the thing talked about — she knew what a fool she'd look if it did.

"But how bitterly she resented our attitude towards it! How callous she thought we were to consider it ghastly instead of touching! How well she knew what we'd do about it when she died — if we only could! So she

put those clauses in her will. Garth represented the future to her, we should have to
put up with Nonie until his twenty-fifth birthday — tomorrow."

"Dismal," said Gamadge. "I sympathize."

"You don't know how dismal yet; you
haven't seen Nonie. A blonde, awful, simpering creature, so like the original that Mother
always said the man had been allowed to take
a death mask. She's sitting at the piano with
her hands spread out on the keys, and one
foot in a white slipper on a pedal. I used to
try to think of it as just a dummy from a shop
window; but I never could. To me it was
Nonie's corpse."

"I feel that way about waxworks myself."

"She has baroque pearl ear-rings in her ears,
and her hair is dressed quite elaborately. The
hair being her own hair makes it worse."

"Much worse."

"Well, Grandmother settled our fate for us;
she was to be mistress in her own house, living
or dead; we had been jealous of Nonie, we
should pay for it. Mr. Allsop was sure to drop
in pretty often to see that we left things as
they were — he knew well enough why those
clauses were in the will."

"Very trying for you."

"Could we be expected to stand it? Even
Mr. Allsop didn't like the idea of its getting

into the Sunday supplements. The Dead Command — that kind of thing; and fancy pictures of Nonie at her piano. We'd just been in the papers, only two weeks before, on account of the Sillerman murder; no, Mr. Allsop didn't object when we told him we were going to seal up the music room. If it was sealed as we meant to do it, nothing in it could be disturbed.

"So we sent off all the old servants except Roberts the morning of the funeral; they were retiring on pensions anyhow. And that evening, before we got another servant in, we made the room vanish."

"Vanish?"

"It has completely vanished. There were seven of us — Uncle and Aunt, Seward and his wife, my father and mother and myself; we made a job of it." She held out her hand for his empty cup, and when he shook his head, went on quietly: "Rowe had gone, as I told you. Garth was only five years old and asleep in his nursery."

"The companion — Miss Fitch; had she retired on a pension too?"

"Not on a pension, but she'd gone; she left after we came back from the funeral in the afternoon. That was the arrangement. None of us liked her, and there was no reason for her to stay."

Mrs. Leeder's face wore, for some reason, a slightly puzzled look; but she did not explain it, and Gamadge remarked: "When the reigning monarch dies, the palace favourites always scuttle off."

"Yes, so they do."

"Tell me how you made the room vanish, Mrs. Leeder."

"It took a lot of planning. We had a conference — I'm afraid you'll be shocked again —"

"I haven't been shocked yet."

"Then I hope you won't be now. We conferred about it the day that Grandmother died; I say 'we'; I mean the older ones, of course. I hadn't much to say about it, but I was more than willing. Next day we shrouded Nonie up in a dust sheet, to look like a piece of furniture, and Seward got in a nice old builder, an old acquaintance of his in his earlier phase as an architect. Seward told him some story about using that top-floor room for storage and protecting it against moths and so on; but the old builder didn't care why we were closing it. He was only interested in the job. He examined the place thoroughly for cracks, and tested the sound-proofing, and listened to Aunt Cynthia explaining that she didn't intend to worry about insects getting in. She didn't; that was quite true. She was going to forget about it until October 22, 1944.

"Luckily there are no electric wires in those walls; the room *was* used for storage until Grandmother converted it for Nonie, and Nonie liked candlelight; there were candle brackets made for the piano. We had a splendid story for him about bricking up the window, and it happened to be true. The will allowed us to dispose of the stables and carriage house next door, and we meant to turn them into studio apartments. We didn't want tenants' children getting on the roofs and breaking that window with their bean-shooters and things. We couldn't have got into the room to repair the glass.

"Well, the builder made a special job of it, and next day he was back with all his materials for sealing; the window wasn't going to be bricked up until later, and it could be done from outside. He sealed the ventilator and the old hot-air register, and sealed the window frames, and inspected the felt strips around the door, and left us the false door he'd made. When he left we unshrouded Nonie."

"Did you? Why?"

Mrs. Leeder smiled. "Aunt Cynthia had an attack of conscience; Grandmother had wanted the room left as it was."

"I see."

"It really was the same, you know. The morning of the funeral we looked about for valuables, but we had no reason to think that there were any; Nonie's ear-rings weren't worth much, and we shouldn't have dreamed of depriving her of them. If we had, I think Aggie Fitch would have had a nerve storm. We didn't naturally consult her about our arrangements, but she hung about and watched them, you may be sure of that.

"Finally we hung a curtain over the window, and went out into the hall, and Uncle Gavan shut and locked the door. And that was the last we saw of Nonie. I wonder if you wouldn't like to see what we did to make the music room vanish?"

"Very much."

She glanced at her watch. "We have time, it won't take a minute. Then we can go into the studio for the end of my story — we often take guests up there, and Roberts will let us know when Uncle and Aunt get home."

Gamadge followed the tall figure into the hall and up to the top floor; a tragic figure, which might have been robbed of its vitality many years before. Tragedy had disrupted her marriage; if she still loved Leeder, it walked with her yet.

The third storey got plenty of the late afternoon sunshine from a big skylight; it could get plenty of air, too — a movable pane in the skylight was fitted with a long iron rod and handle. This hall was as broad as the lower one, with arched doorways, and a cross passage at the east end. Two rooms opened from the passage, and between them was a rather charming wall decoration — a pottery statuette in a niche.

Mrs. Leeder stood in front of the figure, looking not at it but at Gamadge with her melancholy smile. He questioned her with raised eyebrows, and then walked up to the niche; which was not really a niche, but only a section of wall enclosed in an arched moulding like that which framed the doorways. But this moulding had been painted light cream to match the wall-plaster.

The pottery figure was about two feet high, and it stood on a bracket of ornamental ironwork. It represented a water carrier; from his goatskin a cascade of growing ivy poured almost to the ground.

Gamadge asked: "There's actually a door behind that?"

"That is the door, well covered."

"What a clever idea."

"It was Seward's. Not a servant in the house knows that there's a room there; except Roberts, of course. Garth's room is on one side and a storage attic on the other. Who's to take measurements to discover that they don't adjoin?"

Gamadge surveyed the niche with admiration. "You simply kept the door frame and painted it over, and I see that the figure is fastened to the bracket with clamps. The ivy hides them."

"You'll see tomorrow what a thorough job it was. When Uncle Gavan locked the door Seward plugged the keyhole, and then fitted the false door in and plugged the cracks with putty. He plastered over, and painted the whole thing to match the walls."

"Your aunt hasn't lost much sleep over moths and mice, at any rate."

"She was delighted with it. Seward found the bracket and the Italian figure, and put them up. I'm afraid I wasn't of much use at the time, but I'm the one who looks after the ivy."

"No wonder the newspapers never got hold of this. But what an undertaking, with the plaster and what not."

"There was an awful mess," said Mrs. Leeder. "Roberts got rid of the dirt and debris. He'll be on hand again, poor thing, to do the same for us tomorrow. Another mess, and a worse one."

"And what shall you do with Nonie?"

Mrs. Leeder stood gazing at the wall within

the arch as if she were seeing through it into the dark beyond; she said: "You've begun to mix them up too."

"Mix them up? Oh — you mean Nonie and her effigy. It's not so hard, though, to dispose of an effigy."

"They'll probably mash it to pieces in the cellar and throw it away. I think the body is sawdust; just like a wax doll. I don't quite know why it always scared me so; Mother tried to explain it to me at first — how they make those wax images. How they put something with the wax so that it lasts practically for ever, how museums are full of old wax portraits and medallions. It never did any good, I had nightmares. Well, the nightmare is coming to an end."

"What about the bricked window?"

"Oh, that doesn't matter; that can be demolished later on."

"You'll tell the house agent the same story — about the children and the bean-shooters?"

"I don't know what they'll tell him. I don't think it will matter."

Gamadge said: "I assume that the other servants have been given a holiday again."

"Yes, until Monday morning. Roberts is scrambling meals for us to-day and tomorrow, with a little help from Elena and me."

"And who's to demolish this arrangement?"

"Seward and Garth, I suppose. Rowe will be here as one of the beneficiaries under the will, and Mr. Allsop will be here too."

"Everything in order," said Gamadge, smiling at her. "Only one thing left to be accounted for."

"Yes." She turned half away from him. "I'll tell you now why I asked you to come, and to be here when we open the room. Perhaps you'll laugh. It's on account of some buttons."

III

BUTTONS

"Buttons?" In his astonishment Gamadge raised his voice. Mrs. Leeder glanced behind her, past the stairs and down the hall.

"Seward's room is up here," she said. "He and Ena have a suite — the old nurseries. Come into the studio, Mr. Gamadge. I'll tell you there."

"Are my ears working properly?" asked Gamadge, following her to a door opposite the stairs. "Did you say *buttons?*"

"Only buttons."

They went into a long, bright room which corresponded to the sitting-room under it in shape and size; but it had a beamed, sloping roof, and the triple-arched windows were uncurtained and fitted with a cunning arrangement of drawblinds in dark linen. The walls were rough-plastered. There were long worktables, cupboards, racks, and a big easel; but no pictures were on view, and the tables were clear of artists' equipment.

"What a splendid studio," said Gamadge.

"Yes, it is nice. I used to do a lot of pottering here before I was married; so did Rowe. We were always here on rainy days."

"That sounds as if you knew him when you were both children," said Gamadge, diffidently.

"I've known him almost all my life. We went to our first school together, and to dancing school, and we played in the Park."

"So that it was really as an old family friend that your family received him when he — er — came back to the house again?"

"Yes. That made a difference, of course. His mother and father were dead by that time, but we'd always known them. They didn't live far away." She crossed the room to sit on the nearest window seat, and Gamadge sat beside her.

"Buttons," he said.

"A collection of buttons. Grandmother and Aunt Nonie collected them."

"Oh; I see. They were early at the game, weren't they? Now, of course, buttons are all the rage."

"We — the rest of us — knew very little about the collection; we didn't take it seriously, and we had no reason to be interested. Grandmother and Nonie were secretive about their hobbies. They took mysterious motor trips together every summer, and came back with all kinds of stuff that they'd picked up; I'm sure they were the prized patrons of all the famous gift shops in the East. They liked to discuss the trips afterwards, with private jokes and references. I hardly ever saw any of the buttons; I remember some little things like those flower paper-weights that are in fashion again."

"I know the paper-weights," said Gamadge. "I don't know the buttons."

"Do you know whether such a collection could be valuable?"

"It would certainly have a market value nowadays, but that would vary tremendously as the demand for particular buttons in it varied. I don't think there's big money in a button collection, even now; unless some of the items were valuable in themselves."

"Mother said that some of Nonie's buttons had ships and engines on them."

"Association buttons; you'd get a price for them, but nothing like the price you'd get for buttons valuable in themselves — buttons off a rajah's coat, say, or off a king's coat. Jewelled buttons. I know very little about the subject, but I have heard that in the great button period — the eighteenth century — a gentleman could carry quite a little fortune about with him in buttons. The handcut steel ones, for instance, were worth a guinea apiece then."

"Mother says she saw buttons with coloured stones in the collection; it never occurred to her or to us that they might be real jewels. There were cameos, too, and coral ones and ivory ones. How stupid we were. We never thought of the buttons until after the room was sealed up and we opened Grandmother's safe-deposit box. Then somebody did remember them, and we realized that they didn't seem to be anywhere.

"We hunted everywhere, because we began to wonder whether they *were* valuable; Seward's asked dealers about them, and found out a good deal; at least he told us so, but I only know what he said. He said the dealers told him there wasn't much value in the average collection. But . . ." She hesitated. Then she went on: "Personal property like jewellery wasn't tied up in the trust; it was to be divided up immediately among the heirs. We didn't like to think that we might have sealed the buttons up in Nonie's room."

"Oh dear."

"If they were her special treasures, Grandmother might have left them there with her."

"As the Egyptians sealed up personal treasures with the mummies?"

"Exactly. Grandmother had left Nonie's ear-rings in her ears. We began to wonder whether she'd left something else in the room that we knew nothing about; it would have been like her to get Nonie a pearl necklace, for instance, pearl by pearl, on the sly. Her other children were always accusing her of favouritism — it was flagrant."

"Worse and worse," said Gamadge. "Maddening."

"There was one other possibility, of course," said Mrs. Leeder. "Aggie Fitch might have taken the buttons."

"Might she indeed?"

"The room was locked up, as I told you," said Mrs. Leeder, "and Uncle Gavan had the key; he put it in his dresser drawer. That was the morning of the day we had the funeral and Aggie came back to the house with us from Woodlawn that afternoon. She had plenty of time before she left to get the key and hunt about in the music room; at least she may have had — we don't know exactly when she did leave."

"You think she was capable of stealing buttons?"

"We thought her capable of anything small and mean. She was always creeping about and listening. Grandmother found out lots of things she never would have found out if Aggie hadn't told her."

"Was she adequately rewarded by your grandmother for this devotion?"

"We never knew how she was rewarded. She wasn't in the will at all; we thought Grandmother must have been contributing to a fund for her old age — giving her cash presents. That was one of the things that made it impossible for us ever to get hold of Aggie Fitch again, to ask her whether she knew anything about the buttons; we couldn't trace her through her money."

"You mean Miss Fitch disappeared? That looks bad for her."

"She never even communicated afterwards with her relations — some people named Nagle that she used to bring here to see Grandmother; for sponging purposes, I suppose. There was a man and his wife and a sticky little girl; one bumped into her on the stairs," said Mrs. Leeder wearily. "And as Aggie Fitch was some relation of Grandmother's, and the Nagle woman was Aggie's niece, I suppose the Nagles are connections of ours. A horrid thought."

Gamadge said: "We all have Nagles."

"We don't have our Nagles now, thank goodness. They've never been in the house since. The man called up a week after the funeral to ask where Aggie had got to, but we didn't know. He said Aggie had been planning a world cruise, and we finally decided that she'd simply shaken off the Nagles —

since Grandmother wasn't there for them to sponge on, and she didn't care to be sponged on herself. She'd gone off on her own."

"Luggage?" asked Gamadge.

"She'd taken it away with her in a cab the day before."

"She didn't say good-bye?"

"No. You must remember that she had been Grandmother's special property, accountable to none of us; she didn't even have meals with us — she had them upstairs on a tray. We hardly knew that she was in the house, except when she was caught hanging around doors."

Gamadge said after a pause: "You say you did make some kind of search of the music room that morning?"

"We only looked around; we didn't think anything was hidden. What fools we were."

"And tomorrow" — Gamadge eyed her thoughtfully — "you're going to look for treasure in the music room?"

"Yes. Even Elena, though she's not an heir. She thinks it's all a great lark, and so does Garth. They think Nonie is rather a joke, and they're not a bit afraid of publicity. They see it everywhere, all their friends think it's great fun to be in the news. Nonie would never have given *them* nightmares; probably they'd have given parties for her. I think they're better off than we were. Even in my day such things were taken too solemnly."

"Perhaps so. But why am I to be in on this treasure hunt, Mrs. Leeder? I don't understand it at all. Surely you don't need me to help you find the buttons? There will be eight of you, won't there, and a lawyer besides to direct your efforts? Why me?"

Mrs. Leeder was looking out the window. When she turned to him her face was set in an expression of grim resolve. "It will be dark in there, Mr. Gamadge, with that bricked window; even with flashlights and candlelight it will be none too easy to find things; and the more of us there are, the harder it will be. I suggested a lamp on a long wire from the socket in the hall, but they wouldn't bother, and I didn't insist. I kept my insistence for more important matters."

Gamadge said after a moment: "I see the implication. It's a grave one."

"How long do you think it took me to make up my mind about confiding in you — in anybody? What do you think it cost me to admit that I don't trust any of them? But I'm rather alone in the family, Mr. Gamadge; Uncle Gavan and Aunt Cynthia are brother and sister, the last of their generation. They pool their interests. Seward thinks of Elena and she of him. Garth thinks only of himself. Rowe Leeder doesn't put himself forward, he probably won't even go into the music room. They all think that he's only an heir by accident, because Grandmother died; they all think his being mixed up in the Sillerman case killed her. Perhaps he thinks so too, but I know he never in the world would interfere about these buttons. I'm quite alone. Mr. Allsop is too old — he wouldn't see what was happening. If you were there you would see."

"But why should your family tolerate my presence there?"

"They'll tolerate it."

"Have you asked them?"

"No. I'll speak to them this afternoon; I shan't ask."

Gamadge looked puzzled. He said: "What reason have you for thinking that any of them would do such a thing — try to steal the buttons?"

She said: "During the last ten years three objects of value have disappeared from the house, and the servants can't have taken them."

"Oh. I see."

"You can see why their loss was never mentioned to anybody outside the family, least of all to Mr. Allsop."

"You mean that such a loss might have invalidated your right to inherit? The right of you all?"

"We were afraid it might."

"But surely no court —"

"We never dared risk it. We all had too much at stake. But if such a thing could happen three times, why not a fourth? They'll all know why I asked you to come, Mr. Gamadge; they won't protest."

Gamadge smiled. "Perhaps not; but if they don't, they may burst."

"I know it's too disagreeable a thing to ask of anyone; but what if there were pearls? And we all need the money so much."

"What were the things that got stolen, Mrs. Leeder?"

"They were all part of the loot from the Winter Palace of Pekin. Grandfather knew everybody in those days and travelled everywhere, and somehow he acquired the things. The first to go was an ancient seal of the emperors of China; jade, and worth thousands."

"It would be."

"It was kept in a cabinet in the reception-room downstairs; none of us ever thought it would tempt burglars; how would they know what it was?"

"And it would only be saleable in a very special market."

"Yes. I discovered that loss, Roberts the next one: a very old tea-pot, very ugly too. It was kept on a top shelf among the most valuable china, which Roberts washed and dusted himself twice a year. One spring day it — the tea-pot — had gone. There was a great to-do again, but nobody suggested writing to the insurance company. Less than ever did we want publicity; least of all did we want to go to court. And you can imagine how pleasant the situation was at home."

"Very difficult."

"That was six years ago. Then, three years ago, Aunt Cynthia asked me to help her look for some Chinese brocades in one of Grandmother's trunks in the storage attic. A chair in the reception-room was shabby — we never renewed anything if we could help it — and Aunt Cynthia thought she might throw a brocade over it. I noticed that the lock of another trunk was broken, and a mandarin coat was gone out of it. Eighteenth century, I think it was.

"After that we all looked askance at one another; there was a confirmed thief in the house. We never even questioned the cook and maids — too absurd; and poor Roberts was heartbroken.

"But of course we did realize that the thief may have regarded the things as part of his — her — inheritance."

Gamadge asked after a silence: "None of you wondered whether Aggie Fitch mightn't have come back?"

"Aggie Fitch?" She was amazed.

"Well, yes; couldn't she have paid a surreptitious visit from time to time? She knew the house and the valuables, and I suppose she could have retained a door key."

"None of us ever even thought of Aggie Fitch."

"She'd have known there wouldn't be an outcry."

"I wish it were true."

"She may never have gone farther from you than a bus could take her in an hour. Those Nagles, Mrs. Leeder — where do they live?"

"Heaven knows. I think they used to live in Jersey City."

"Didn't anybody ever suggest any theory at all to exculpate the Clayborn family?"

"Uncle Gavan and Seward did try to suggest something, but they never dared quite put it into words to *me*."

"Mr. Leeder?"

"Yes. Rowe Leeder isn't a thief."

"Why did they suggest him?"

"Because he had been so very poor, and because he began to come back to the house just before the emperor's seal was taken — or at least missed."

"He knows about these stolen things, and about the buttons?"

"Yes. He's always known about the buttons. Grandmother and Nonie used to show him lots of their hoard; he gets on with anybody. It's a great gift. People don't irritate him, they just amuse him; even Aggie Fitch did."

"He is uncritical?"

"I don't think he's ever taken in; he simply doesn't think it's ever worth while to be annoyed."

"Then he's mistaken."

"I'm not good at analysing people; I don't want you to misjudge him. You'll meet him this afternoon — if you still intend to stay."

"I'll stay, and no matter how much my feelings are lacerated I'll come tomorrow."

"I do thank you."

"But I can't help feeling, Mrs. Leeder, that you're a courageous woman; to bait your relatives like this."

She was surprised. "I'm not afraid of them."

"Evidently not."

"They'll be angry, but they'll restrain themselves. Would they like me to confide in Mr. Allsop instead of you?"

"They'll prefer me if they think I won't tell."

"They're clever in certain ways, very clever. They'll probably see for themselves the kind of person you are, and I'll try to make it clear to them."

Gamadge said: "I'd better remind you that you can't make people believe you're in earnest about a thing unless you are in earnest. *Would* you confide in Mr. Allsop if they refused to let me in tomorrow?"

"Yes. It was bad enough to lose the other things and say nothing. When I think of them, all crowding into that room tomorrow — the bad light, the confusion — I don't feel that I can stand it. I've thought about it; I've had a long time to think about it. Tomorrow, even if it is Sunday, is the day specified in the will for the trust to come to an end. I don't believe that even Mr. Allsop would make difficulties for us now that it's all over."

"But the others wouldn't face the possibility of his making difficulties in the matter of those things stolen from the house?"

"They're terrified of a lawsuit. They want the money now. So do I want the money, I don't know what I should do without it. But Uncle Gavan and Aunt Cynthia are old, and Seward isn't strong, and he has Ena to think of."

"Garth?"

"The very idea of losing the money would send him off his head. Garth won't risk anything."

"He and Miss Elena Clayborn are out, so far as the thefts are concerned, I suppose."

"Elena certainly is; when the emperor's seal disappeared she was only eight or nine. I don't know what Garth was capable of at fifteen. He wouldn't have been able to dispose of the things without help. I'm inclined to think that he knows nothing about them."

"On the score of youth, not of character?"

"You'll see him, Mr. Gamadge. Perhaps I'm prejudiced. He wasn't a very nice little boy."

"One thing, Mrs. Leeder — didn't the rest of the family have the same opportunity that Miss Fitch may have had to take those buttons out of the music room twenty years ago?"

She looked startled. "We were all here, and my father and mother and Seward's wife besides; but the button subject came up so naturally. It never entered my head . . ."

"The other things hadn't been stolen then. By the time they were stolen you were used to the idea that the buttons were still sealed up with your aunt Nonie, or gone with Miss Fitch."

"I suppose so."

"So — other considerations aside — your father and mother and Mr. Seward Clayborn's wife may be ignored in the matter of the buttons because they had died before the other things were taken."

"Yes. You can ignore them anyway. Seward's wife was such a gentle little thing, and my father and mother . . . ."

The mild old voice of Roberts came to them from the hall: "Miss Harriet, the doorbell has rung."

"Thank you, Roberts. Give us half a minute. Nobody will blame you for being a little late to-day." As she and Gamadge left the studio she added: "But they wouldn't bother to use their keys before ten o'clock at night, no matter how much Roberts had to do."

"My old Theodore would never let us hear the end of it if we didn't use our keys."

"This family is spoiled, frightfully spoiled."

She and Gamadge were settled in their old places, before a tall man and a tall woman came into the sitting-room. They were elderly people, but they conveyed a strong impression of vigour, activity, and communion with the outside world.

Mrs. Leeder said: "Hello, you're late for tea. Let me introduce Mr. Gamadge. Mr. Gamadge, my aunt Cynthia and my uncle Van."

IV

CLAYBORNS

Miss Clayborn and her brother had the kind of offhand manners that are civil and easy, but hardly manners in the formal sense at all. "We have got beyond all that nonsense," they seemed to imply, "and so no doubt have you. You are to take us for granted, and if we couldn't take you for granted you wouldn't be here."

They might hardly have noticed him as an individual; but Gamadge was sure that in the very moment of introduction they had taken in his appearance, his clothes, his behaviour, and penetrated beyond to his probable station in life. Gamadge thought he was accepted.

He relinquished his place to Miss Clayborn, and sat down at the other end of the sofa. Gavan Clayborn drew up an armchair in front of the tea table, so that across it he faced the fire. He and his sister were tall like Mrs. Leeder, but blue-eyed and sanguine of complexion; Gavan — who on closer inspection looked at least seventy years old — was broad and thick in the shoulders, with plenty of grey hair and a cropped grey moustache. He wore faultless clothes carelessly. By the look of him he had lived well, but had had plenty of hardening exercise. Gamadge thought he might be moderately amiable, satisfied with himself, and immovably selfish.

Miss Cynthia Clayborn was gayer and more raffish. She wore smart tailored clothes, a fur — sable — and a tall, feathered hat. Her shapely feet were shod in high-heeled pumps. She seemed competent and tough.

She settled herself against the cushions of the sofa and remarked in a harsh voice that it was a nice day. Mrs. Leeder had already poured tea for her uncle, and handed him his cup. Roberts came in with a salver on which stood a stiff highball in a cut-glass tumbler. He set it down on the little table near Miss Clayborn, then lifted Sir Arthur Wilson Cribb out of the way.

Miss Clayborn snatched the solander from him, opened it, and took out a cigarette. Gamadge lighted it for her. She said: "You'd better have what I'm having, Mr. Gamadge."

"I refused one, thank you all the same."

"I need it. Great Heavens, that endless music. Gavan, aren't you joining me?"

"Had plenty at the club."

"I bet you did. How was the game?"

"Fair, until a man cut in we didn't know well."

"Win all your money in the last rubber?"

"No, and didn't like losing. Bridge isn't supposed to be a source of income at that club."

"Oh, come now," said his sister.

"I said isn't supposed to be. Membership isn't watched nowadays." He turned a casual blue eye towards Gamadge. "Do you find that so where you play?"

Something had mysteriously told Gavan Clayborn that Gamadge was not poor and not rich; he already knew it, knew it finally, but Gamadge's reply might establish his rating more accurately. Gamadge obliged: "The stakes we play for wouldn't do much to our incomes one way or another."

"Much better to keep them moderate." Half a cent, thought Gavan.

Mrs. Leeder asked: "Was the music so very boring, Aunt?"

"Oh, Heavens. I don't know why Elena or you will never go, and let me off."

"They'd rather have you."

"There was the usual appeal for funds in the intermission. They won't get any more from the Clayborns. I hope the man noticed my old fur."

"He probably noticed your new hat."

Miss Clayborn squinted up at a drooping plume, dyed in shades of mauve, wine colour and purple. "Nobby, isn't it? You ought to have seen the other ones. Do I look like a woman who would be likely to have pansies on her first autumn hat? They still try to make me do it. When we sell the house I shall have a fur cape." She addressed Gamadge: "Somebody wants it for a girls' school, Mr. Gamadge. Perfect, with the garden and the studio."

"Perfect for you, if you think so," said Gamadge, "but sad for the rest of us — these changes. Once an old house passes out of a family, anything can happen to it."

"I should be quite willing to stay on," said Miss Clayborn, picking up a sandwich and biting into it. She swallowed the bite, and went on: "If I had a million dollars. As it is, how shocking it will seem to pay rent."

"As shocking as taxes?" Gamadge smiled. "I'm hanging on to my small old house."

Clayborn said: "Much better if you can."

"I use it as an office too. That makes a difference."

Clayborn looked inquiring; but just then a tall, very thin man with dark hair and eyes and a long oval face came slowly into the room. Mrs. Leeder said: "Mr. Gamadge, my cousin Seward."

61

Seward behaved as if he were depressed and tired. He nodded to Gamadge, took a cup of tea from Mrs. Leeder, and walked over to the window at the right of the fireplace. He sat down on the window seat, put his cup on the cushion beside him, and got out a cigarette.

"Mr. Gamadge," said Mrs. Leeder, "has a most interesting occupation. He's an author too —"

Seward glanced at Gamadge with pale interest.

"But his real business is most interesting. He finds out all about old books and papers. It's like being a detective; forged documents and that kind of thing."

Gavan Clayborn, suddenly alert, stared at Gamadge with open surprise. "Gamadge? Gamadge? Haven't I heard —"

"By your expression," said Gamadge, "I'm afraid you have."

"The Gamadge we've seen in the papers?" asked Miss Clayborn, with tolerant wonder.

"Unfortunately I have been in the papers."

"Those cases!" Miss Clayborn was more and more flatteringly kind. "What fun!"

"Well, not entirely."

"Shouldn't think you could stick it," said Seward Clayborn.

"Stick anything if you get mad enough," said Gamadge.

"Right, absolutely right," agreed Gavan. "Don't do to be too squeamish in these days."

"Never did to be too squeamish, perhaps."

"I'm too squeamish," said Seward in a tired voice. "Much too squeamish."

Mrs. Leeder said: "Mr. Gamadge is the one person in the world — I think you'll agree with me — whom I could ask to be here tomorrow when we open the music room." And as Gamadge gripped the arms of his chair, she went on: "To find the buttons."

There was a profound silence, during which Gamadge relaxed. Then Clayborn said shortly: "Don't understand you," and his tea slopped in his saucer. No; Gamadge wasn't going to be thrown out.

"He's entirely discreet," continued Mrs. Leeder calmly, "and he doesn't bungle. If the buttons are there he'll find them in no time."

Miss Clayborn, ignoring Gamadge, looked at her niece. "Harriet," she asked in her harsh voice, "have you gone stark crazy?"

"No, Aunt Cynthia, I haven't. Anyone would tell you that it's much better to have an impartial person present —"

Seward's cold voice interrupted her. "Harriet, you really have gone out of your head. Mr. Allsop —"

"Mr. Allsop is about eighty, and what does he care about the buttons? *They're* not

63

part of the trust."

Another silence followed. Gamadge broke it, speaking mildly: "I know how you must all feel; it must seem like an intrusion, and unless you can accept it it will be an intrusion. But may I suggest that a disinterested referee takes responsibility from the parties involved and makes things simpler for all? You engage me to find the buttons; I find them if they're there, all of them, and place them in Mr. Allsop's hands for sale or distribution. No delay, no argument. I should like to tell you about my Great-aunt Myrtle."

They were all looking at him now; Mrs. Leeder quietly, as one who has done her part and leaves the rest to a stronger ally. Clayborn's face was unreadable; but while his colour was high, his sister's had faded until her conventional makeup stood out against her pallid skin like camouflage. Gamadge, turning his head to include Seward Clayborn in the conversation, was greeted by a stare of almost ludicrous consternation.

Gamadge crossed his knees and lighted another cigarette.

"My Great-aunt Myrtle," he began, "was a peculiar and terrifying old lady with a weak heart, who lived with her brother — until he died — in a large old mansion in a country town. She was not, I may remark here, terrifying to me; I used to spend a month of my summer vacations there when I was a boy, and we got on very well.

"She knew that when the brother died the house and property, and all the old family stuff in the house, would go to his children. She had money of her own, and would be comfortable; but naturally she didn't look forward to the move, and she very much disliked the eldest son's wife.

"Her brother died one spring, and she was allowed the summer to pack and arrange her affairs. She couldn't have stayed on, too many servants were required there for her means; and she wouldn't have dreamed of sharing the house with any of the heirs.

"She had unfortunately got it into her head that certain items in the inventory belonged to her personally; and those items, to the dismay of the heirs, began to disappear. There was little doubt that when she left they would leave with her, in her trunks and boxes. It was a delicate situation: nobody wanted a scandal or a lawsuit, and nobody wanted to be accused of having killed her — she had a heart attack whenever the matter of the lost items came up. She said that they had never been in the house at all, or that they had disappeared long before, or that Great-uncle must have given them away. The fact was, of course, that she had settled it with herself —her right to the objects — but didn't dare submit her cause to earthly justice.

"The objects were valuable, and they were heirlooms; some silver, a piece of lustreware, and a coral necklace. The necklace was antique and beautiful; fifty-one carved, matched, graded beads, ranging in size from a pea to a chestnut, and with a bloom on them that I can't describe. Great-aunt Myrtle knew who wanted to wear *that*, and she couldn't stand it.

"Finally, in despair, the family got her own lawyer — a small-town crook if there ever was one — to ask her whether she'd allow an impartial person, duly authorized, to make a search for the things. They — and he, I think — hoped that would scare her. Great-aunt Myrtle said certainly, only she would pick out the impartial person. She thought it was a tremendous joke on them all when she picked me — I was thirteen years old at the time, and still with her on my vacation. She said I was the only impartial member of the family that she could think of — our branch didn't inherit — and that whatever I found I could turn over to the bank which represented the estate.

"The heirs were distraught at first; but my father and mother, knowing my propensity to plod, were amused. They wrote and told the others to leave it to me.

"I of course considered the hunt an indoor sport of the first magnitude, and the fact that I wasn't to be paid" — Gamadge paused here a moment and looked at the end of his cigarette — "didn't dishearten me in the least. The first thing I found, sensibly enough, was her bunch of keys; and I unpacked and repacked her trunks in the attic with the greatest care. I also did a good deal of climbing and ladder work, ripped and pried things up as neatly as I could, and didn't neglect the hints that I had been given by Edgar Allan Poe and Sherlock Holmes.

"Of course the family row had been conducted over my head, and I thought the hunt was approved on all sides. When I found the coral necklace in the course of my activities I didn't find it in one piece, but in fifty-one pieces; each bead separately; and as I discovered a bead I would place it with some pride in a glass jar on the sitting-room mantel — where Great-aunt Myrtle and I could both look at the results every evening. I shall never forget the curious expression on her face as she sat and gazed at the bloomy growth in the jar.

"Her worst error, poor thing, lay in forgetting that her heart attacks affected me very slightly. She had one or two when she looked at the jar of coral beads, and I was sympathetic; but if she had given up the ghost at my feet I shouldn't naturally have felt guilt or remorse.

"Well, all the things were found. The heirs wanted to give me something really monumental as a reward, but my father and mother wouldn't allow it. They said I had been chosen because I was impartial, and impartial I must remain."

After a silence Miss Clayborn said in her rough, metallic voice: "Very amusing. But I don't see that it applies to this matter, unless you wish us to believe that Harriet isn't paying you for your services."

"But even that, if it were a fact," said Seward's voice in a drawl, "wouldn't prove Mr. Gamadge impartial. Harriet has many friends of all sorts. I don't think any of them would be impartial in a case like this."

Clayborn's face was still suffused with blood. He said in a growl: "Allsop will say whether any of us is to be allowed to import strangers in an estate matter."

"But I should ask Mr. Allsop to supervise my labours," said Gamadge. "Much easier for him to supervise one person than eight."

"And do you think it would be wise, Uncle Van," asked Mrs. Leeder, "to take Mr. Allsop

68

into our complete confidence even now?" She added: "After tomorrow, perhaps we can all engage detectives if we like. Regular detectives. But we shouldn't be able to trust them as we can Mr. Gamadge; *he* won't give us away — even to Mr. Allsop."

Miss Clayborn looked at her for some moments in silence. Then she said in a lower key: "You've been pretty quiet about it, all these years, Harriet."

"About what, Aunt Cynthia?"

"About your feelings — how you felt towards us all."

Gavan Clayborn sat with his chin sunk into the folds of his speckled scarf, his hands grasping the arms of his chair. Gamadge thought that ten years before he would have exploded into violent speech and action; now he was too old, and Roberts was too old to back him. But as the front door slammed below, and a commotion shortly followed on the stairs, he said: "Garth will have something to say about it."

"Garth!" Seward's tone was ironical and weary.

"You needn't keep squashing the boy and belittling him," said Miss Clayborn, turning her head to scowl at her nephew. "He can't help it if he has a weak chest. All the Clayborns are not robust, as you most certainly ought to know."

"I was thinking of his mental equipment," said Seward. "Mine is still functioning at twice his age."

"There's nothing the matter with Garth's mental equipment," said Mrs. Leeder, "except laziness and too much alcohol."

A young man and a young girl rushed into the room, but paused at the sight of the visitor. Mrs. Leeder, with a glance at Gamadge which seemed to him a little guilty, said: "Why, Ena! What became of the party?"

"It wasn't a good party," said the girl.

"Rotten party," echoed the young man.

Miss Clayborn took the introduction upon herself. "This, children," she informed them in a mincing tone, "is a Mr. Henry Gamadge. He's a policeman. Harriet invited him to be here tomorrow to see that none of us pockets those buttons."

The two stood nonplussed for a moment, and then the girl came forward, her brilliant teeth showing in a broad smile, and offered Gamadge her hand.

"Mr. Gamadge isn't a policeman," she said. "He's a book detective. I always wanted to meet him. Mr. Gamadge, how's David Malcolm?"

Gamadge, with an enlightened smile at his client, shook hands with Elena Clayborn and said that Malcolm was very well.

"He was the nice boy that came to lunch," Elena reminded her father. "The one that had the headaches."

"He doesn't have them now," said Gamadge. "I'm the one that has them."

"A charming young man," said Elena's great-aunt. "Very civilized."

"Mr. Gamadge is his boss. What did you mean, Great-aunt, about the buttons?"

Elena Clayborn was tall, and had the predominant Clayborn build. Her bright blue eyes were full of sparkling gaiety, and her colour was healthy and high. Luxuriant brown hair curled beneath a small hat that matched her autumn tweeds.

Garth Clayborn now advanced. He did not look like a Clayborn at all; he was below medium height, with narrow shoulders and a narrow chest. His features were small, and he had a sickly skin.

"Yes, what's the joke?" he asked. "Everybody knows that Mr. Gamadge is a great man."

Gamadge said "Thanks," laughed, and shook hands with him.

"Did you think we were going to snatch the buttons?" asked Garth, laughing too.

"Mrs. Leeder had the sensible idea that it would simplify matters if one person looked for them — one person at a time." He added: "I mean, of course, with all the rest of you looking on. I shouldn't take on the job, naturally, unless I could have all of you, and Mr. Allsop, watching *me*. Mrs. Leeder thought a little order and formality might expedite the proceedings."

Garth cast a somewhat puzzled look — not an amiable one — at Mrs. Leeder; but he said: "Not a bad idea," and wandered off down the room, while Elena joined her father on his window seat. "Less of a scrimmage," continued Garth. "The fun will come later, when we're all able to throw the junk out of the windows — the junk we hate most. I'll start with this." He seized the thick stem of a brass floor-lamp, which was topped by a red shade as big as an umbrella, and heaved one claw leg off the floor. "Many's the time I've barked my shins on it," he said.

Elena declared loudly: "I'm going to be there when you open the family vault. Garth says I can't."

"Certainly you can't," said Garth, setting the lamp down. "You're not in on the clan secrets. You weren't born when Nonie was tombed up."

"I suppose you were in on it? In your creepers?"

"Perhaps I was. I was a most intelligent

child, and I took in a lot that was going on." He strolled across the room, glanced at the things on a table, came back to the stand at the end of the right-hand sofa, and opened the cover of Sir Arthur Wilson Cribb. He took out a cigarette and lighted it. "You have my permission to be present tomorrow, Mr. Gamadge," he said, "and if you like you can have a slice of my birthday cake. But if you're going to be here, you'll be required to assist at the exhumation. Bring your own crowbar."

"You are apparently the man who could not shudder," replied Gamadge.

"Shudder at Nonie? I look forward to meeting her."

"Do you think she'll be well preserved," asked Elena, "or will she crumble into dust like the mummies?"

"And are we going to bury her in the cellar?" asked Garth.

"Children," said Miss Clayborn, "you are disgusting. You have no decent feelings whatever; but Ena might remember that her father is one of the people whom Harriet suspects of wishing to steal the buttons."

"As I get it," said Garth, "Mr. Gamadge is merely going to act as referee."

"Mrs. Leeder and I," said Gamadge, sitting down again at his end of the sofa, "are less and less sure that the buttons will prove to be in the sealed room at all."

"Oh — Aggie Fitch," said Miss Clayborn.

"And I even produced a theory that she may have returned from time to time and taken the other things that seem to be lost."

At this there was a pause. Then Garth said abruptly: "If I'd been more than five at the time, I'd have had a thorough search made that evening when the room was sealed. Then there'd be none of this nonsense at all."

Gavan said shortly: "When we need your opinion on that matter, my boy, we'll ask for it."

"My opinion is," said Elena, "that three mysterious men and a boy came and took the emperor's seal and the tea-pot and the mandarin coat. Like *The Moonstone*. They were all stolen goods — *we* had no right to them."

"Psha," growled Gavan.

"I like the Fitch idea," said Seward in his slow way. "I like it very much. Didn't you women think she picked up trifles where she found them — knick-knacks and essences?"

"Her people were a very poor lot," said Miss Clayborn. "We thought they — or that little girl they brought — picked up things. I dare say they knew very well where Aggie got to."

"Never did understand how Mother could

tolerate the little creature," muttered Gavan. "But she valued ties of blood."

"So did the Nagles," said his sister dryly. "Cousin This and Cousin That. But she made herself useful, Van."

"Humoured Grandmother too much," said Seward. "I imagine that if all were known we'd find she was responsible for the wax museum. What a relief to be rid of it."

Garth had walked the length of the room to the west window. He stood at the left looking out to the street; then he turned. "Leeder wasn't here, was he, when the room was sealed?" He asked it thoughtfully.

"No," said Mrs. Leeder, casting an angry glance in his direction.

"He's coming along now up the street."

"Oh, good," said Elena. "I can't live without my Roly-poly."

She was out of it, Garth didn't seem to care; but Gamadge thought the three elder Clayborns had powers of restraint and recovery to a remarkable degree.

V

LEEDER

Mrs. Leeder said: "Rowe called me up about the time he ought to come tomorrow. I asked him to drop in to-day, because I wanted him to know that Mr. Gamadge was going to look for the buttons. I know you're all very angry with me, even Garth, though he pretends to take it so coolly; but you're not to take it out on Rowe Leeder."

Gavan, sunk in his chair, answered without looking at her: "Do you think we haven't discussed him, Harriet, in connection with those thefts — which you've seen fit to discuss with Mr. Gamadge? We all thought he made off with the button collection."

"I didn't," said Elena. "Imagine him taking things and selling them!"

Gavan sat glowering at her. He said: "Needed the money. He got no allowance from your great-grandmother's will; when it was made he had a salary from his firm. Remember that. Gad, the fellow gets all the women. If it hadn't been for your great-aunt

Cynthia I wouldn't have allowed him in the house again."

"He took good care to wait until Harriet's people were dead," observed Seward. "Ena, I wish you wouldn't keep up this absurd pose of yours; it's perversity. You must always take the other side."

"Leeder had only been gone a couple of weeks when we sealed the room," said Gavan. "I never heard of his turning in his latch-key before he left. And he was broke afterwards — somebody at the club says he saw him driving a taxicab. The murder case he was mixed up in shows what kind of company he'd been keeping — even after his marriage."

Mrs. Leeder said: "You're very moral all of a sudden, Uncle Van — for a Clayborn."

"We observe the decencies."

"And Rowe wasn't mixed up in the murder case."

"Oh, pooh!" said Garth from his distant window. "That alibi. Those three cronies of his would perjure themselves in a minute to keep a classmate and a club member out of the electric chair."

"And they dropped him afterwards," said Seward. "Don't forget that."

"Because there was publicity," said Mrs. Leeder in a choked voice. "Because that janitor talked to the papers. It was only by an accident that anybody ever knew —"

"Anybody but those friends of his," said Seward, "and the police. If the police had to choose, which do you think they'd choose as the probable thief in a family — Leeder, or one of the rest of us?"

"That's so unfair," said Mrs. Leeder. "So unfair."

"Question of character," said Gavan. "I'm not talking about the murder; they're always saying that a murderer needn't be any other kind of criminal, though I think that's nonsense. But that woman was mixed up with the underworld, where they'll do anything."

Garth said: "Well, I never objected to Leeder coming here; he's a valuable fourth at bridge. If I could always have him for a partner I'd never lose."

Miss Clayborn rose. She said: "It's not for you to object to Rowe Leeder's presence here, Garth; please remember that a sixth of the house and a sixth of the estate belongs to him."

She toddled from the room on her high heels, as the front door slammed. Garth asked in a lower voice: "What does he do now, anyway? Where does he live? Anybody know? Do you know, Harriet?"

She replied indifferently: "No. He never talks about himself."

There was silence until a tall, thin, dark-haired man came quietly into the room. The lids of his grey eyes drooped a little, which fact gave him a quizzical expression that matched his smile. His features were as thin and sharp as beaten metal, but there was nothing beaten down about his manner. His pepper-and-salt clothes were well made, but more than well used; they were almost seedy. His hands were in his pockets as he smilingly surveyed the room.

"Mr. Gamadge," said Mrs. Leeder, "let me introduce Rowe Leeder."

Gamadge rose and returned Leeder's nod.

"Mr. Gamadge is coming tomorrow to find the buttons, Roly," said Elena.

"Buttons? Oh, the collection. I should think that would be soon found, if it's there." Leeder came up to the end of the sofa, opened Sir Arthur Wilson Cribb, and took out a cigarette. He lighted it, pulled up a chair, and seated himself as Gamadge also sat down. "Quite a lot of the things," he went on. "Poor old Nonie showed them to me once. Can't say I was much interested, but I thought some of them were pretty. Nonie had them all poked into pockets in a case."

"Were there jewelled ones, Roly?" asked Elena.

"I dare say. I don't remember. I just thought they were some of her gimcracks."

"Is Roberts bringing you something?" asked Mrs. Leeder. "Or shall I ring for more tea?"

"Not a thing, thanks," said Leeder. He looked up at Gamadge. "You a button authority?" he asked. "Going to value them? I thought you were a book man."

"And a crime man," said Elena. "He's just going to look for the buttons, so there won't be a scrimmage in the music room."

Leeder cast a sidelong glance at Gavan Clayborn, and then looked at Gamadge again. "Well," he said, "if you all think that's the best way. Poor old Nonie. It'll seem funny to see her again. I always felt rather sorry to think of her walled up in there. The place for family skeletons is in the open, where they can rattle themselves to pieces."

Gavan rose heavily from his chair, and without a look at anybody walked heavily from the room. After a moment Elena said: "He's wild, Roly."

"He would be, if Harriet wished Mr. Gamadge on him." Leeder smiled at Gamadge. "What's the idea? That the buttons are hidden in some inaccessible place?"

"My idea," said Gamadge, "if I can be said to have one, is that they're gone."

"Aggie Fitch must have taken them," said Elena, "and she must have taken the other things."

"Well, I never thought so," said Leeder. "Timid little peeper. I think her adventures stopped at reading letters. She used to give mine a going-over now and then; I didn't mind. She had few pleasures."

"But then who did take the things?" asked Elena, looking at him anxiously.

"Oh, these mysteries — they're never solved. Somebody breaks something or loses something — takes something out of the house to show a friend and mislays it, or the friend does."

"Takes three things?" asked Seward.

"It's all too vague and too long ago," replied Leeder, "and it's a good-sized family. The things might turn up yet. The big mystery to me is how Harriet persuaded Mr. Gamadge to take on the button job."

"You think it an unlikely job for me?" Gamadge, rising, exchanged a long and inquiring look with him.

"From what I seem to have heard of you," replied Leeder, getting to his feet, "I shouldn't have thought it would commend itself to you much."

"It commends itself to me." Gamadge leaned across the tea table to shake hands with his client. "What time tomorrow?"

"Three o'clock. And thank you again so very much."

"I'll be here."

He nodded from one to another of the people in the room, and went downstairs. Roberts, warned by some bell, was waiting for him. The old servant's face was a friendly blank; Roberts had the invaluable gift of knowing secrets without betraying the fact that he knew them.

"I'm to be at the opening tomorrow, Roberts," said Gamadge.

"Yes, Sir?"

"Don't let them badger Mrs. Leeder to death before I come."

"No, Sir," said Roberts gravely.

Gamadge, in fact, was not entirely easy in his mind about his client. As he walked down Fifth Avenue along the green old wall and then past the Museum, in a chill dusk that smelled of smoke and leaf mould, he wondered if it was fantastic of him to be uneasy. Her position was an isolated one; the young people had no authority in that house, Leeder had less than none. Would they, even if they cared — and Garth probably wouldn't care — know how to protect her? Did *he* know how? What could he do about it if he should be refused admittance tomorrow, told by Roberts in all good faith that Mrs. Leeder had been taken ill?

Gamadge allowed his imagination free rein. Gavan Clayborn and his sister were tough-minded people, how tough Gamadge didn't know; Seward Clayborn looked and behaved like a warped and a disappointed man; Garth was physically and morally weak, but perhaps he had a strong sense of property. They had all four of them been forced into proximity with one another and the Leeders by the restrictions of a will; they were all poisoned and embittered by mutual distrust and suspicion.

Mrs. Leeder was standing between them and — what? Leeder would presently go home, wherever that was; Elena would eventually go to bed. If old Roberts should be told that Mrs. Leeder had been seized with an illness, would he telephone to a stranger about it? Would he even be tempted to do so? He was devoted to them all; if he had abetted her this afternoon he had done so as he would have abetted her in some innocent plot when she was a young girl.

Mrs. Leeder might lie under drugs for days. Something could in the end be done about it, but what would Gamadge be able to do on the spot, tomorrow? He had no authority, no standing, and nothing to act on but the airiest hypothesis. Mrs. Leeder herself dreaded publicity, she had depended on him to keep the whole thing a dark secret. He could disregard her wishes if her own safety should be in question; but no policeman would force his way into a house without a search warrant, certainly not a house like the Clayborn house, and on what could Gamadge base a request for a search warrant now, before the fact?

By the time he had reached his own street and turned east, he remembered that Mrs. Leeder was not afraid of her relations.

"I'm a fool," he told himself; "she knows them better than I do."

On reaching home he went directly to his office, which had once been the Gamadge drawing-room. He got out an encyclopedia, and was finishing an article on buttons when Malcolm came through from the dining-room, which was now the laboratory.

Gamadge scowled up at him. "Thanks for the job you found me," he said acidly.

"Job?"

"Elena Clayborn turned up and gave you away. What do you mean by pushing this Clayborn thing on me while I'm on leave?"

"Ena just said Mrs. Clayborn wanted advice."

"If I'd known you two juveniles arranged it, I wouldn't have gone up there."

"That's what I was afraid of."

"Now I've got to go back tomorrow."

Malcolm leaned against the edge of the

desk. "Why did you take the job if you don't want it?"

"I was afraid not to, damn it. What kind of treatment do you think I'm getting from those barbarians?"

"I thought they were a charming family," protested Malcolm. "Except Garth, of course. I rather think that that fellow looks upon me as a little black man."

"A what?" Gamadge considered the height and elegance of his assistant in some surprise.

"That's a term they use at the seat of learning he patronized — for types they're not accustomed to."

"You must have been very rude to Garth Clayborn," said Gamadge.

"I thought his behaviour to Ena was oafish; I may have let him see that I thought so."

"You may." Gamadge studied him. "How well do you know this Clayborn girl?"

"Didn't you like her?"

"She seems very nice. She must have got it from her mother."

"But her father's a most delightful man; cultivated and gifted. He does beautiful work."

"I didn't meet him in the most auspicious circumstances. Don't bring Elena Clayborn here to the house unless I say so."

"Why not? It's exactly what I meant to do.

I want her to meet Mrs. Gamadge," said Malcolm.

"Don't bring her here until I give the word. You've made the Clayborns my business; in this case I prefer to keep business out of the home."

Malcolm said after a pause: "I like Ena Clayborn better than any girl I ever met."

"Of course you do; she's a fountain of vitality. How about the Lucas girl, who thinks she's got you cold?"

"Ellie Lucas thinks nothing of the kind. I got you up there to advise Mrs. Leeder because Ena asked me to. Surely you think Mrs. Leeder's charming?"

"She is. Consider yourself in on the case, if it is one, and tell me what you know about the family."

"Nothing, except the Leeder tragedy. Everybody knows that."

"Certainly a tragedy for Miss Sillerman."

Malcolm looked taken aback. "Ena says he was completely exonerated. Did you meet him? I thought he was perfectly —"

"Charming. So did I. Leeder the Mystery Man. What do you know about the case?"

"Only that this Sillerman woman was shot, and Leeder's name and address were in her telephone book; but lots of other men were in her telephone book — only the janitor of

her flat saw Leeder go in there the night before. Recognized his photograph. He talked
to some newspaper, and Leeder got into the
headlines — the other men didn't."

"There is no justice."

"He had an alibi; he was playing bridge with
three friends at his club."

"Private card-room?"

"I don't know."

"What did he say about having been to call
on Miss Sillerman the night before she was
shot?"

"Said she was an old friend of his bachelor
days, and that he just dropped in. Of course
it was a big scandal."

"Even he wouldn't be surprised at that."

"He behaved very well, considering the circumstances. Had an interview with the old
lady, packed his bags and got out."

"But returned."

"Ena thinks he was worried about his ex-
wife. Ena says the family's rather down on
her. Thought she should have got out too,
married somebody else, taken the scandal
away from the house. Ena says they're pretty
hard-boiled — her great-uncle and aunt. She's
very fond of Mrs. Leeder. Thinks it's wonderful of her to have stuck by him. At first
she couldn't — too much pressure for a young
woman of twenty-four or so. But she never

did marry again."

"Why didn't she marry Leeder again?"

"Ena says he wouldn't consider it."

"Looks upon himself as a man forbid, does he? He seems to bear up medium well."

"That's his disposition. Ena says he's a stoic."

"Touching. What was the Sillerman girl like, do you know?"

"Bad lot. Hadn't worked for several years, lived in an expensive flat with a cook and a daily maid, had all kinds of jewellery and furs, and invested money."

"Anybody suggest at the time why Leeder should have killed her?"

"No, unless she'd been blackmailing him and he got tired of it."

"Does he hold himself responsible for old Mrs. Clayborn's stroke, and subsequent death?"

"Ena thinks he does, and that that's why he never had the energy to break away and start fresh and make any money."

"He must have made enough to live on, unless he'd saved or had a private income."

"He hadn't a thing. Ena says he only laughs when she asks him what he does for a living, and tells her it isn't for polite ears."

"He's accepting his share of the estate, however, in spite of the possibility that he isn't morally entitled to it?" And as Malcolm did not answer, Gamadge added: "Perhaps remorse is a luxury stoics don't permit themselves. I forget. Elena's view of him is romantic."

Theodore came in and stood waiting at the door. Malcolm said: "He's had a thin time of it for twenty years. Of course everybody dropped him; of course they said he'd only married Harriet Clayborn for the Clayborn money."

"Well, I suppose they thought that if he continued to drop in afterwards on his girl friends he couldn't have married for love."

Theodore said: "Excuse me. Cocktails are served. And I remember that case, Mr. Gamadge."

"You would."

"*You* was in college; but your father and mother, they was deeply interested in that murder. Everybody in New York said Mr. Leeder killed the young person, and was lied out of it by his friends."

"That's always the more interesting theory."

"Too bad," said Theodore. "Young feller, came from nice folks that lost their money. They was dead, and he lived in clubs and kited around. Big doings when he married Miss Harriet Clayborn, what a couple they made.

Everybody wanted to marry Mr. Leeder, but he would have Miss Clayborn. It was a love match."

He turned to go, and then stopped.

"Mr. Leeder and that showgirl," he said. "That was all part of the foolishness of those days. You don't remember, Mr. Gamadge — you was in college. Those was the wild days. Speakeasy right next door to us, folks climbin' over our yard fence when the place was raided, trucks drivin' in from Canada at four in the mornin', all full of murderers. Young people runnin' crazy. Shootin's everywhere. Bootleggers invited to folks' houses to dinner."

"I get the picture," said Gamadge. "I was in college, but I wasn't dead."

"Mr. Leeder got in too deep," said Theodore, "and he shot his way out."

"Part way out." As they left the office Gamadge addressed Malcolm: "Wasn't the Lucas girl to be here? What happened to her?"

"She went home. Mrs. Gamadge couldn't get a fourth for bridge, and it wouldn't be any fun for her to stick around, just talking."

"Oh, wouldn't it?"

VI

COLLEAGUE

Gamadge, walking along the Clayborns' street on the following afternoon, reflected that it would probably be no quieter twelve hours hence, at 3 a.m. on Monday morning, than it was now. By five o'clock exhausted people would be pushing baby carriages through from the Park, children of the East Side would be straggling home; now the sun warmed empty pavements, not a car stood at either kerb.

He paused to look up at the bricked window. He now knew that Nonie sat beyond it in the dark, at her piano. He wondered how close to madness old Mrs. Clayborn had been when she called that image into being, while she sat alone beside it through the years. Could she have survived those vigils without at last coming to believe that there was more to her companion than sawdust and wax?

He thought that the will had been based on some such unrecognized delusion. Mrs. Clayborn had made her favourite child live on, surrounded by her treasures. It must have taken courage to rob her, with her mother only just laid in the grave.

He went along to the front steps, mounted them, and rang. Yesterday's impressions had faded, he was no longer apprehensive enough to feel relief when Roberts invited him in. Roberts looked a little solemn, as if a funeral might be going to take place instead of a disinterment.

He said: "If you would just step into the reception room, Sir, before you go up. Mr. Allsop would like to speak to you." He placed Gamadge's things on an oak chest, and led the way to an arched doorway on the right.

Gamadge entered the grand, faded, dim-lit apartment, beyond which could be seen through an arch a great, shining, oval dinner table. Afternoon light fell upon the long expanse of Aubusson carpet, upon the folds of green brocade at the windows, the malachite mantel, the gilt cabinets. There was a concert-grand piano here, there was a portrait above the chimney piece.

Mr. Allsop got up from a small sofa to the left of the fireplace, and advanced a few steps across the scrolls and garlands beneath his feet. He was a dry little old man, but there was alertness in the pale old eyes behind his pince-nez.

He put out a small, dry hand.

"Mr. Gamadge?"

"Mr. Allsop."

"We might sit down."

They faced each other from opposite sides of the tiled hearth. At the end of Gamadge's sofa there was the inevitable stand, this one gilt with a malachite top; and on it was a vellum-bound royal-octavo volume, which Gamadge eyed knowingly. Its red edges had certainly been glued together. He smiled, lifted the cover, glanced within, and asked Mr. Allsop if he smoked gold-tipped cigarettes.

Mr. Allsop looked benignly at the solander. He said: "Very clever. Very ingenious."

"But poor old Dante, though." Gamadge, holding the box shut, examined its spine. "*Divine Comedy, III.* I hope it was an odd volume. I must ask Mrs. Leeder if Hell or Purgatory is missing."

"Would she know?"

"She and Mr. Seward Clayborn used to make these things."

"Oh, then it would be an odd volume. Or pages would have been out. Seward is not the man to destroy a valuable book. I know them all." He observed Gamadge through his glasses, lifting his chin to get a good view of the other's features. "A wonderful family. My father first brought me here when I was

93

quite a child; I was allowed to play in the garden. A Paradise, I thought it," he said, smiling at the cigarette box. "Quite a Paradise. We had the usual brownstone, with our laundry drying in the yard."

"I suppose this house was brighter then; before the apartments went up across the street."

"Brighter in every way," said Mr. Allsop. "Spacious living, contacts —" He got out his handkerchief and tapped the end of his nose with it. "Contacts," he repeated, putting the handkerchief away, "all over the world. Distinguished company. Lavish hospitality." He peered up at the portrait above the mantel; a handsome blonde woman who looked obstinate.

"Didn't do her justice," said Mr. Allsop. "The fellow didn't get her at all. Fashionable man then, they tell me he's gone out of fashion since. Mrs. Clayborn was a woman of great charm and character, but she had losses. Not financial losses, I am glad to say; she escaped all that. Her great pride was the Quartette, and I have tried to watch her posthumous interests. I — er — took the liberty of looking you up, Mr. Gamadge, as well as I could in the short time at my disposal, after Mrs. Leeder telephoned me yesterday evening."

"I'm glad she did that."

"She — er — had a reference; a Mr. Macloud. Mr. Robert Macloud. There is no better trial lawyer in town."

Gamadge said dryly: "Her own sources of information must have been extensive. She only knew me at second hand when she asked me here."

"Well," said Mr. Allsop, "Mr. Macloud is always on the side of the angels; from the point of view of the Bar Association, I mean."

"I must tell him you said so."

"You may. I thought at first, when Mrs. Leeder telephoned me that she had asked you to be here on this occasion, that she would have been wiser to consult me."

"Naturally you did."

"And I was very much surprised to hear from her," continued the old gentleman, lifting his chin again to look at Gamadge down his nose, "that the family made no objection to your coming. The older members of it are clannish and conservative, Seward is sensitive and fastidious, Garth has always had a great idea of the Clayborn importance. The sealed music room and its contents have been a jealously guarded secret. I may say now that I was not in favour of sealing the room at all. But I could not protest effectively, and it was done under my own eye."

"Such a secret, of course," said Gamadge,

"can be a source of power — can be used as a threat."

Mr. Allsop said: "I thought it on the whole a mistake. There might have been a certain amount of talk, but nothing to the talk that would arise if the fact of the sealed room came out afterwards." He glanced at Gamadge. "From what Mr. Macloud told me, I do not think it will come out through you, Mr. Gamadge."

"I don't think it will. Excuse me for asking this, Mr. Allsop: didn't you think it a mistake that there should have been a wax image in the first place?"

Mr. Allsop reflected. Then he said: "I see no harm in discussing the matter with you. I heard nothing of the wax image until it had been set up; then I did reason — as tactfully as possible, for she was in a distressed condition of mind — with Mrs. Clayborn. I begged her not to be governed by morbid fancies. She argued the matter with me, I may say, sensibly. She reminded me that portrait busts and statues, of every conceivable material, are made and placed in private homes as memorials every day. Coloured wax images of saints and madonnas are set up in churches abroad, their costumes changed and jewellery hung upon them; and nobody thinks of them as morbid. Nonie was her saint.

"I would not have you think, Mr. Gamadge, that I failed to talk the matter over with her physician. He assured me that the image would prove to be a solace to Mrs. Clayborn, that she was entirely sane about it and was likely to remain so, and that he wouldn't answer for the consequences if she were badgered about it."

"But then you found that she had made a will, forcing the image upon the family for many years."

Mr. Allsop hesitated. Then he said: "I was not a young man myself at the time, I was in fact approaching sixty. My sympathy was already with the old. It was within my knowledge that the family had not been considerate in their attitude towards my client when she lost this favourite child. I thought it not too grave a burden to put upon them, since my client was leaving them all her money, and nothing more to her Quartette. I don't like such wills — they're a lot of trouble, and this one has been a trouble and an anxiety to me." He looked about him, smiling. "I was prepared to be lenient in my interpretation of the restrictive clauses; I have been lenient. I have done no hunting about for infringements. I have not watched the length of the family vacations. I have not, in effect, persecuted them. When they wanted to seal the room I acquiesced, as I say. But why, now that the secret has been preserved until the very day when it need be guarded no longer — why should the Clayborns condone this — excuse me — intrusion of a stranger?"

He waited, heard nothing from Gamadge in reply, and went on: "Mrs. Leeder told me why she had asked you to come, and I was astounded. I can only think that she may be suffering from a mild case of persecution mania. Leeder . . ."

He paused, and went on more briskly: "There is another explanation, perhaps. She might have been afraid that Leeder would abstract these buttons."

"Leeder?"

"You are surprised; she stands by him with pathetic fidelity. But does she trust him? Can she do so?"

"I don't know him, Mr. Allsop. I can't say."

"You know his history?"

"In outline."

"It would of course be most unfair of Harriet to pretend to you that you are here for the purpose of protecting her against the others, while all the time she is dreading some sleight of hand on the part of Leeder. But women can be subtle, and they can be unfair."

"As part of the human race," agreed

Gamadge, with a smile, "they unfortunately can."

Mr. Allsop smiled in return. "I say these old-fashioned things; quite out of date. Well: if there is any question whatever of losing the buttons in such a way . . . Can they be of great value, Mr. Gamadge?"

"Not unless there are jewelled buttons among them; and even so —"

"Even so, why should they tempt any of these people, who will receive their inheritance — a substantial sum for each — in a very short time?"

"I hardly know. Mrs. Leeder seems to think that the buttons — any extra value — might be a temptation to the heirs. And she even wonders whether Mrs. Clayborn may not have hidden something of greater value in the room."

"What she put there will be found. I take no stock in this nonsense about Agnes Fitch. Agnes Fitch was a harmless and devoted person, quite incapable of theft, I should say. Families, Mr. Gamadge, always dislike these humble satellites; but they can't do without them. As for Miss Fitch taking herself off without notifying anybody, I can only say that elderly drudges, when they find themselves free at last and with money in their pockets, often do take themselves off. They get a frenzied sense of personal liberty. Something was said about a cruise; she went on the cruise, and who knows what happened to her and to her travellers' cheques? Extraordinary things happen to unprotected spinsters and their travellers' cheques."

"Did you know these relatives of hers — the Nagles?"

"I don't think I ever saw them. Well." Mr. Allsop rose. "I gather that you will go first into the room —"

"You and I will," said Gamadge, with a smile.

"You and I. I may say that I don't like the notion of Leeder barging about in the music room looking for concealed property. He may even know where the buttons are; that poor girl that died was devoted to him."

"He seems able to inspire devotion."

"As a lawyer," said Mr. Allsop, "I have nothing against him. As a human being, and strictly in confidence, I hate the sight of him. He was certainly the cause of that stroke which cost my client Mrs. Clayborn her life, and I am quite sure she would have made another will, cutting him out, if she had been able to do it. And though he inherits with the others, who knows what his expenses may be? When he was a young man, I can assure you that he always provided himself with the best.

He has ruined Harriet's life, yet he has the impudence to come here. Unfortunately he has a certain legal standing."

Gamadge, after a pause, asked: "Tell me, Mr. Allsop: did the police ever do any work on that alibi of his in the Sillerman case?"

"None. What took them off his trail and kept them off it was the drug complication. The Sillerman woman dispensed narcotic drugs to certain clients. When that came out, it widened the inquiry to embrace the entire underworld, and the murder was attributed to some disappointed drug addict or pedlar." Mr. Allsop took a step or two towards the door, and turned. "You don't feel free to tell me why, in your opinion, the Clayborns accepted you, Mr. Gamadge? No? Perhaps it's as well that I shouldn't know what compulsion Harriet has laid upon her relatives. I shall go up now and tell them that I think it's best to humour her."

"Thanks very much."

"Roberts will notify you when the matter has been adjusted."

The old gentleman trotted off, was met in the doorway by Leeder, gave him a short nod, and turned in the direction of the stairs.

Leeder came into the room smiling. He said: "Poor old boy," and approached Gamadge at his easy gait. His hands were in his pockets,

101

and when he leaned up against the mantel shelf he kept them there. Gamadge had never met anyone before who used fewer gestures or seemed able to maintain one attitude so long without changing it. He was like one on whom quiet has descended for ever.

He asked: "Has *he* accepted you?"

"Having been warned that there might be some irregularity in the proceedings this afternoon, he accepted me naturally. Any lawyer would have done the same."

"Irregularity." Leeder's eyes, under their drooping lids, studied Gamadge curiously. "You did stir them up with that story of yours about the coral beads. Did you invent it for that purpose?"

"No, it was a fact. There are queerer facts in my experience, in everybody's."

"Poor Cynthia intercepted me on my way out yesterday to tell me about it and ask me what I thought about it. She's wondering whether you intend to rake over the music room for pearls from a hypothetical pearl necklace."

"I didn't bring a rake, or any implement but a torch."

"Too bad that Harriet felt she had to make all this commotion. There's a magpie in the house," said Leeder. "A hoarder. No theft intended, since the lost articles belong to all.

Probably the loss will be made up later when the legacies are paid up; some unobtrusive adjustment. Such loot is never found in a house if there's no organized search; it's moved from place to place."

Gamadge said: "If the buttons are found, we might have to face the possibility that the other things were taken by one of the young people."

Leeder raised his eyebrows.

"Never too young to be a magpie," said Gamadge. "And the history of the objects might be an additional attraction."

"That's a charming theory. Why not extend it?" asked Leeder. "If the buttons are not found, I mean. Kleptomania in the family, handed down from one generation to the next — or the next but one. I ought to embrace the idea — it lets me out. Well, you're here, full of useful theories; but why are you here?"

"You know why, Mr. Leeder."

"I know what Harriet's asked you to do; and I wish she hadn't. She's allowed the family to get on her nerves. They've been getting on her nerves for years, and this is the final blow-up. But what I should like to know is, how did she persuade you to take on the job? You're a busy man and a man of standing. You probably are not at all used to the kind of thing Gavan and Cynthia and Seward must have treated you to in the way of manners."

"Would you have expected me to go reeling from the house?" Gamadge smiled at him.

"Not if you were determined to see it through. But why were you so determined to see it through?"

"I have my natural quota of curiosity."

"Perhaps. I shouldn't have thought it would lead you along such by-ways as this one."

"It leads me along strange paths. I might ask *you* a question, Mr. Leeder, if I wanted to risk offending you."

Leeder was amused. "I don't take offence."

"Then why did *you* come back?"

"You mean to-day? I'm legally in on it."

"I mean ten years ago."

Leeder moved for the first time. He stepped forward, took a cigarette out of Dante's *Paradise*, and lighted it. Then he held it out towards Gamadge. "This kind of thing."

"Free cigarettes?" Gamadge smiled.

"All the fleshpots. Food and drink are served opulently to all comers. Have you ever eaten regularly in drugstores?"

As Gamadge continued to smile at him sceptically, he went on: "And light conversation. Everything kept light. These people are one's own people; it's relaxing. Nothing painful discussed — not even buttons, until

Harriet broke the rules. Nothing real."

"That makes it restful?"

"As a day in the country. Old Gavan, poor old buffer, what's his life? His club, his stockbroker, somebody else's yacht. Cynthia plays bridge with her cronies, nothing changes for them; they're as important to one another as they always were, and they do the things they've always done. Seward lives in his studio, still trying to paint like Renoir — on the sly."

"Mrs. Leeder?"

Leeder frowned at his cigarette. "Harriet travels a lot, or did. She oughtn't to have been here as much as she has been since the war. Nerves, just nerves."

"Who wouldn't be nervous with valuables going out of the house under Allsop's nose?"

"I don't think the old boy would have done anything."

"He has a great sense of his responsibility towards his late client."

"One thing," said Leeder, "I'm convinced of. There's nothing of value in the music room unless the buttons are there and are valuable. They'd have told me."

"Who?"

"Old Mrs. Clayborn and Nonie. If Nonie had a pearl necklace, she'd have told me. They let me in on their secrets — they knew I wouldn't give them away, even to Harriet. I knew from the day Nonie died that there was going to be a wax figure; I was nothing but a kid in school, but Mrs. Clayborn told me that. You know I'm glad the poor girl died before her mother. God knows what would have happened to her if she'd lived — she was nearly thirty years old, and had the mentality of sixteen. No place for her in the world."

Elena came rushing into the room and seized Leeder's arm. "Come on," she said, "you two. They're all up there waiting to begin."

"As one of the heirs," said Leeder, as she dragged him towards the door, "I protest against your being in on this. I won't have your great-aunt Nonie made a show of to little brutes like you."

Gamadge stopped in the hall to get his torch out of his overcoat; then he followed them upstairs.

VII

"SHE HAS MOVED"

Gamadge found the top storey bright with sunshine from the skylight, and its east end full of people. Three of them, however, were somewhat dissociated from the rest; Mrs. Leeder stood against the wall beyond the stair-head, while Leeder and Elena Clayborn, like supporting statues, faced each other from either side of the studio doorway. Leeder seemed to be keeping his young friend where she was entirely by the power of the eye.

Roberts was laying newspapers in front of the section of wall that masked the hidden door, and had already covered several yards of carpeting along the corridor. An empty wooden crate and a basket of tools stood on newspapers beside the stair-well railing. To be out of the way, the rest of the group had withdrawn to right and left of the masked door; Mr. Allsop, Gavan Clayborn and his sister on the right, Seward and Garth on the left. Both of these last were in slacks and shirtsleeves.

Roberts finished his job and stood up. He asked: "Would you wish me to stay, Mr. Clayborn?"

"No, thanks," said Gavan. "We'll ring when we want help in clearing away."

"I have more baskets ready, Sir."

"All right. Good." Gavan spoke shortly; he looked angry and baffled, and he held a large bronze key in his hand, gripped tight.

Roberts went down the hall. He opened a door some few yards beyond where Mrs. Leeder stood, and went through it, closing it after him.

Gamadge maintained himself at a polite distance from the center of the proceedings, against the stair rail.

Seward stepped forward; he looked bored with his job, but he had a workmanlike air. He carried a big screwdriver.

"Take the statuette, Garth," he said. "I've unscrewed it."

Garth lifted the pottery figure with its mass of trailing ivy, and carried it into the studio. Then he came back and stood beside Seward, who was working on the bracket.

"Want help?" he asked.

"No. It isn't as much of a job as it was to put them in."

Garth held the bracket until it was free, and then walked off with it and deposited it also in the studio. He returned to find that Seward had picked two chisels and two hammers from the tool basket. He handed Garth one of each.

"Lightly, now," he said. "You get the library steps and work from the top. If we crack the plaster away in big pieces there won't be so much of a mess."

Garth brought the steps. In a short time the whole thin coat of plaster was cracked and peeled away, exposing the wooden surface of the false door.

"Shall we clear off?" asked Garth, looking down at the fragments of plaster around his feet.

"Not yet; we have the putty to get out. Tough stuff, that wood putty, but it'll chip out."

The edges of the false door were sealed with a substance that came out under the blades of the chisels like sections of hard wood; but the sections were long, and the work went on fast.

Mr. Allsop cleared his throat. "No doubt," he said, "some of the others would be glad to assist."

Seward answered shortly: "Thanks, it won't take long. This is the worst of it. Only a minute or so more."

At last he inserted the blade of the chisel

into the thin crack that ran up the left side of the false door. Garth lifted the steps aside, and returned to shove his own chisel in. The whole inset moved, and fell forward. Garth caught it in his arms.

"Gad, that was a nice piece of carpenter work," said Gavan. "Look at it come! Smooth as glass."

Garth carried the big arched slab down the hall and set it up against a door frame. Then he came back, and he and Seward shovelled debris into the crate. Then he dragged the crate away, while Seward crumpled up the newspaper and its dust and wadded it into the tool basket.

"Well, I must say!" Miss Clayborn was impressed. "I wish I'd known that you two were so handy around the house."

"Men can do everything better than women can," said Garth, who seemed eager and excited. "If they want to."

"Yes, that's the catch," said Miss Clayborn.

"What I plan the construction of I can demolish," said Seward. He stood looking at the dark and polished panelling of the oak door that now stood exposed. "Not even marred, and we can get a man to take the cream paint off the moulding. Garth, hand me that spike you'll find in the basket."

Garth fumbled about under the wadded

newspaper, and produced a wooden-handled spike. Seward took it, examined the plugged keyhole, neatly removed the plug, and stepped aside.

"All right, Uncle Van," he said.

Gavan moved forward, key in hand; but Mr. Allsop was in front of him. He said: "I take over now, Clayborn, as we decided."

Clayborn hesitated. Then, without a word, he gave Allsop the key.

"Our plan," said Allsop, "is in the circumstances the best one to follow." He spoke dryly, with authority, and with a whole lifetime's experience behind him; experience in reconciling differences between recalcitrant heirs. "Mrs. Leeder, one of the residuary legatees under the will of my client deceased, has provided an agent — a man, I may again inform you, of the highest reputation and ability — to look for objects of value in this room.

"I propose to unlock and open this door, enter the room — somebody will kindly provide me with a torch — and stand aside. Mr. Gamadge will then go in, light the candles if necessary, and conduct his search alone. The family, and Mr. Leeder, will remain on this side of the threshold; but the doorway is wide, and they will be able to see exactly what he does and finds. So will I."

Leeder spoke calmly from where he had propped himself: "Ena and I won't obstruct the view. We'll stay here."

"And I shall stay here," said Mrs. Leeder.

"Then there will only be four to watch the proceedings," said Mr. Allsop. "Quite enough."

Seward was now looking very tired; he had got out his handkerchief and was wiping his forehead with it. "You understand, Allsop," he said, "that Harriet has forced us into a position where we can't protest without compromising ourselves?"

"My boy," said Mr. Allsop coolly, "what I understand or do not understand has, I suppose, no bearing on the matter in hand. Let me simply say that I shall be very glad indeed to get the whole thing over with as quickly as possible. You have all waited a long time for your money; I shall have great pleasure in handing it over to you as soon as the law allows. Now if someone will hand me a torch . . ."

Garth took one out of the pocket of his slacks and passed it over.

"Thank you. Mr. Gamadge?"

Gamadge walked down the hall, torch in hand. He stood waiting while Mr. Allsop put the key in the lock and after a short struggle turned it.

Seward spoke dryly: "Might I make a suggestion?"

Allsop, his hand on the bronze door-knob, paused and looked over his shoulder. "Certainly."

"By this time the place will be practically a vacuum. Mightn't it be as well for Garth to open the skylight before you go on? Then you could wait until the air gets in."

"Of course. Excellent idea. Of course."

Allsop straightened and looked up at the skylight. Garth dragged the steps into position, mounted them, and reached for the handle of the long rod. He turned it and pulled; a big triangular pane slowly descended on creaking hinges, and was followed by a surge of cool air.

"Good." Mr. Allsop turned the knob and pushed. The door opened from left to right inwards, and he went into the room with it. Then he came scuttling back. "Good Heavens!" he gasped.

Gamadge, at his left, and with the torch in his hand still unlighted, saw nothing for the moment but the dark sheen of the curtain over the window; he too stepped back, as Miss Clayborn, who had pushed up to the doorway, shrieked: "Why, it's awful! *Can* a rat have got in and died there after all?"

Gavan growled over her shoulder: "Nonsense. No worse than a closed cellar. Garth, Ena, hurry now. Go and open all the windows on this floor, but keep the door of the servants' wing shut. We'll have the place aired in no time."

Garth and Elena ran, Leeder silently disappeared into the studio. By the time he had returned the whole corridor was swept by a fresh autumn breeze, and the peculiar deadness from the music room had given way to something more breathable.

Mr. Allsop stepped in again and stood to the right, Gamadge advanced from the left and put on his torch. What he saw was so grotesque and startling that for a moment he could only stand staring at it. The wax figure, demurely clad in its white dress, with its yellow hair and its simpering smile, was in itself mildly horrifying; what made it terrible was the fact of its having been swung about on the revolving piano stool to face the door. Its hands, spread out as if playing upon a keyboard, now clutched the air with crooked fingers that looked ready to claw and rend.

Miss Clayborn shrieked again: "O God! She has moved."

Gavan, Seward and Garth had crowded up. Gavan said after a moment of consternation: "The piano stool's been turned, that's all."

"Turned? Turned? When?" Miss Clayborn

was stammering.

"When Aggie Fitch stole the buttons," said Seward. "They must have been in the piano. The figure was shoved around to be out of the way. No use looking for anything in there now."

Gamadge alone, from his position within the room and to the left, could see the right-hand corner. When his torch cast its beam there it stopped. He said: "Please keep back, everybody. Do you know what Miss Fitch was wearing the day she left?"

"Wearing? Wearing?" Miss Clayborn glared at him. "What do you mean? She was wearing an old grey caracul Mother gave her."

"And a red hat?"

Miss Clayborn simply gazed at him as if she thought he had gone mad. Allsop, his torch forgotten, was peering around the edge of the door and clinging to the knob. Nobody spoke until Mrs. Leeder's shaken voice came to them from down the hall: "She had a red hat and a red dress on at the funeral."

Gamadge said: "Then she never did leave. She's been here ever since."

Mr. Allsop came staggering back to the doorway, and Gamadge put out an arm to steady him. He said: "She's on the sofa there. Nobody must go in. Nobody must touch anything. Gamadge, shut the door."

But Gavan had already forced his way past him. He stood looking into the corner, his broad shoulders hunched and one hand opening and closing rhythmically. Miss Clayborn, her face yellowish, had retreated until she was back against the opposite wall. Seward stood as if helpless, his arms hanging. Garth danced about, trying to get into the music room, trying to see.

Mr. Allsop, recovering himself admirably, spoke with finality: "Clayborn, come out of the place. We must send for the police."

Gavan did not seem to have heard him; but when Gamadge went up and touched him on the shoulder he turned without a word and came into the hall. Gamadge pulled the door shut, and Mr. Allsop turned the key.

Garth asked excitedly: "But what killed her? Why should we send for the police until we find out what killed her?"

"Because we're told to," said Seward, with a short laugh. His face looked bluish. Elena had come up to him and was trying to persuade him away from the locked door and down the hall. He hung back. "Harriet brought a witness in," he said. "Somebody to tell us what to do."

"If you think for one moment —" began Mr. Allsop severely, but broke off. "No, of course you don't, Seward. You're all of you badly upset. There is only one thing for us to do, and we must do it now. Mr. Gamadge will go down and telephone for the police. And in order to relieve us of responsibility, I'll ask him to take this key with him."

Elena said: "Come along, darling, you're not able to stand. Come and lie down. I'll stay with you." Seward shook his head.

Garth persisted in repeating questions which no one seemed able to answer: "But how could it have happened? Did she drop dead? Was she sealed up alive in there by accident?"

Gavan shot him a furious look. "Don't be a fool. Sealed up? The window wasn't bricked for days afterwards."

"She got in there somehow after you locked the door, and you never took a look again?"

"Why should we?"

Gamadge took the key from Mr. Allsop and went along the hall to the stairs. His client, standing white-lipped and motionless, addressed him soundlessly: "I've been stupid."

"No."

"Did you expect this?"

"I did think of it as a vague possibility, when you told me that Miss Fitch had disappeared."

"And that," said Leeder from the studio doorway, "is why you decided to come back to-day, isn't it?"

"That's why. Mrs. Leeder, where's the telephone?"

"There's only one, in a back passage off the first-floor lobby."

Gamadge went down, found the telephone, and called the precinct. He asked for Detective Lieutenant Nordhall.

VIII

SIR ARTHUR WILSON CRIBB

Some two hours later, at approximately six o'clock, Lieutenant Nordhall sat at a broad oak writing table beside the south window of the Clayborn library. He was looking up at Gamadge, who had perched himself upon the opposite end of the table and was smoking a cigarette.

The library, which ran the whole east length of the house, represented more outlay in time, money and labour than all the rest of the rooms put together. It was ceiled and walled in black oak, which had been imported in slabs from a manor in England. Most of the furniture had been imported with it, and the low glassed bookcases that lined the west side of the room had been built and carved to match.

Its north and south windows could not light it even at midday, and Nordhall had a green-shaded student lamp to work by. Papers lay in front of him, and near them a cardboard box that had held writing paper.

He and Gamadge had been very thick for

several years, since they had worked together on another case; but he had always rather hoped to catch his friend at a loss. Now, grinning up at him, he spoke merrily:

"They got a long start on you this time. Twenty years' start. Motive lost in the pawnshops of twenty years ago, and the corpse is a mummy. We don't want the Medical Examiner, we want to send down the Avenue to the Museum. They have professors there that can tell whether prehistoric remains had their skulls beaten in, or whether they were just trephined by the local medicine man."

"Skull beaten in? You said she was strangled."

"So she was." Nordhall cast an affectionate look at the cardboard box. "And we didn't find any buttons."

"Then there are none there. They must have been in some sort of tray or case lying on the piano wires."

"Yes, but were there ever any buttons? I'd like to know why this Aggie Fitch was killed. I'll ask you to come up with me later and look the place over."

Gamadge was not enthusiastic at the prospect: "Why?"

"I'd hate to miss anything. Had enough of it, did you?" Nordhall laughed. "But it's nice up there now, nice and airy. You'll like it now.

The boys poked some of the bricks out of the window. We've got a high-powered lamp trained in from the hall; the body's gone, the sofa's gone, and the waxwork's gone too. Just wax head and hands and a sawdust body. Want to see the head?"

He lifted newspapers from something on the window seat beside him, and placed the something on the table.

"Had to look for buttons inside it," he said. "We took the hair off and the eyes out."

Nonie's head, bald and eyeless, seemed slightly less repellent to Gamadge than before. Perhaps it *had* been a death mask; now it looked like one.

Nordhall asked, gazing at it: "Was the old lady nuts?"

"They say not."

"I'd say the girl was. Flat-headed, and a silly smile."

"She could play the piano." Gamadge got off the edge of the table and wandered across to one of the low bookcases. He glanced at shelves and passed on to the next; in no room that contained books could he have refrained from looking at the books. Nordhall went on talking:

"The jewellery she had on wouldn't cost twenty-five dollars in a store, and I don't think it would sell for ten. The old lady wasn't leaving anything of much value in there."

Gamadge picked up a quarto volume from the top of a bookcase, smiled at it, brought it over to Nordhall and opened it. He asked: "Have one?"

Nordhall peered in at gold-tipped cigarettes. He said: "Well, I'll be switched. What will they think of next?"

"This isn't a new idea; the house is full of them. Mrs. Leeder told me she and Seward Clayborn used to make these boxes." He closed the solander and looked at the label: "*A Season in the Cotswolds. By Lady Athenia Lewis, 1802.* Fine old mottled calf, but badly eaten by the acids in the colouring. Too bad." He walked back to the bookcase and bent down. "I think I see another friend, know him anywhere by his spine." He drew Sir Arthur Wilson Cribb out from between two other books on the shelf, and brought it to the table.

Nordhall glanced at it without interest. "Funny," he said, "to put it in among real books."

"Yes. Funny." Gamadge was smiling.

But Nordhall frowned. "You mean it was put there on purpose? Why?"

Gamadge perched himself on the edge of the table, the solander in his hands. "Yesterday," he said, "when I arrived, this thing was in the sitting-room upstairs, on the table beside my sofa. Mrs. Leeder offered me a cigarette out of it, and I referred to what it had partly been about — when it was a book. It had contained a chapter on the Assassins — the Thugs — of India. They were much talked of when Sir Arthur wrote his journals, and he naturally wrote about them too."

"Well, what about them?"

"They were a religious brotherhood, worshippers of the Goddess Kali. They went about strangling people from behind, according to a ritual, while under the influence of hashish."

Nordhall stared.

"The method seldom failed," said Gamadge.

"It wouldn't. Not much harder than tying a parcel, if you could get behind your party." He continued to gaze into the greenish eyes of his colleague. "You talked about this with Mrs. Leeder?"

"A word or two. Mrs. Leeder had apparently never read Cribb's journals before they were converted."

"How about the rest of the family?"

"Nothing was said about Cribb."

"But they saw you using it?"

"I didn't use it after the rest came, but some of them used it."

"It belongs up there in the sitting-room?"

"Yes. When Garth came in he looked for

123

it on another table, where there's a lamp and smoking materials."

"None of them knew you were coming. Did they know who you were — that you'd be likely to know about a book of that kind?"

"Yes, in a general way."

"One of them knew — the one that knew there was a strangled corpse upstairs, and that you'd be in on the discovery. That party hoped you hadn't noticed the Cribb book, didn't want you seeing it again and noticing it. So it was brought down here and put among all these other books, best place in the world to hide it."

"The leaf in the forest?"

"That's right. No questions asked at a time like this if it got mislaid for a few days. But if it had been got rid of after the Fitch murder — when was it made, do you know?"

"Years before the room was sealed, before Mrs. Leeder was married."

"Exactly. It had been sitting around the house for years, and if it had disappeared then it would have been missed and questions asked. This party had applied the Thug methods described in the book; didn't know but that somebody else in the family might have read it. Better to leave it around as usual, no questions raised about it, nothing done to fix it in anybody's mind. People like these

124

Clayborns would forget all about it.

"But you were different. If you noticed it, good-night. You'd be pretty likely to know all about this Cribb, and these Thugs, and put two and two together, and draw the conclusions we're drawing now. Your best friend couldn't have been sure you'd see the Cribb book in this library to-day."

"No."

Nordhall slapped his hand on the table. "By gum, Gamadge, you're always useful."

"Thanks."

"Who but you would have noticed the title of the thing in the first place, or known what Cribb wrote about, or seen it just now in that bookcase?"

"Lots of people."

"Don't be meek, when you're meek it always means you're pleased with yourself."

"You seem to be pleased with me."

"Because you've placed the Fitch murder definitely in this house, and definitely in this family, and included Leeder."

"Why should you ever have imagined that the Fitch murderer wasn't inside the circle?"

Nordhall laughed. "Ever hear of some people called Nagle?"

"I have, yes."

"They're connections of the Clayborns. Fitch was related to Mrs. Clayborn, and Mrs.

Nagle is Fitch's own niece. Clayborn and Seward and Miss Clayborn have all had me aside to tell me all about these terrible no-good Nagles. They knew the house, they may have known that Fitch had her savings on her in negotiable form that day, she may have let them in by the back stairs.

"I got hold of the Nagles."

"Good. How?"

"Clayborn got his full name for me out of his mother's papers, Elbert T. Nagle. Being Sunday made it a little harder, but not much. Having his office address, we could send down and find the janitor of the building — it's an old rat-hole of a place. He opened up, and we got Nagle's home address, Jersey City. Nagle's a kind of a theatrical agent in a small way, his office is a den in a suite. The Nagles will be along any time now.

"I talked to him on the telephone. Sounds a wise kind of guy in a cheap-sport way. He's going to identify the body, if you can call it identification — we got most of what we needed in that line from Miss Clayborn; clothes, so on. The interesting thing is that the Nagles didn't make much of a fuss over Fitch's disappearance. But they don't interest me so much now, because they weren't here yesterday and didn't hide Cribb.

"Now about Leeder. Did you know he was

around the house a good deal when he was a boy?"

"Yes."

"His folks lived just down the Avenue. He had plenty of chances to read all the books in the house, often stuck around on rainy days and read in this library. Played around with Seward and Mrs. Leeder — Harriet Clayborn then — in the studio upstairs." Nordhall gave Gamadge a sidelong look. "I have a nice little piece of evidence that fits in there, and it helps to eliminate the Nagles, too."

"Can't you give it to me?" Gamadge returned the smile with a bland, hurt look.

"Little surprise I'm saving for you. It'll make Mrs. Leeder feel confidence in me when she finds out that I haven't been telling you everything first. I wouldn't like her to think we were in cahoots."

"That would be a mistake," said Gamadge, looking astonished.

"You bet it would. You're a witness, not a pal. Keep that in your head. Mrs. Leeder is still your client, luckily for her."

"Luckily? Because I found Cribb in that bookcase over there?"

"That's why."

"She wouldn't thank me for keeping the murder in the family, would she?"

"You've put it on somebody that didn't discuss Cribb with you, and that ought to suit her. About Leeder, there's one thing in *his* favour. The Sillerman woman was shot."

Gamadge blinked, and then said: "So she was."

"It's not much to go on, because amateurs don't always repeat methods the way professionals or crackpots like to do; and besides, the Fitch murder may not have been planned in advance. But it was premeditated."

"Was it?"

"You bet it was; part of my little surprise for you. So was the Sillerman murder premeditated — a .38 calibre revolver isn't usually carried around in people's clothes. They never found that gun, of course, but they have the bullet still. Case was never closed, you know. They're sending up the files for me to look at."

"One more thing in Leeder's favour," said Gamadge with a smile. "Mere trifle. He had an alibi."

"Yes — three friends. I wasn't old enough to be in the Department then."

"You'd have gone pretty carefully into that alibi?"

"I don't say it wasn't gone into. Anyhow, I'd like to see those files."

"I'd like to see them myself."

"Remind me." Nordhall leaned back in his chair. "Seward Clayborn, now — not so good. He'd know where to find a market for that collection of buttons, knows all kinds of art people. I wish I knew whether there ever were buttons in that music room. Miss Clayborn had some sort of a story of yours about finding coral beads in fifty-one places."

Gamadge laughed. "I was just calming them down, so that they wouldn't make too much of a row about my coming to-day."

"Yes, and I have a couple of questions to ask you about that. And I'd like to know what their reactions were when the body was discovered. All you say is they acted naturally."

"They did. They acted according to their characters."

"One of them had twenty years' practice. Want to know something?"

"Very much."

"If you hadn't been there they'd have buried Fitch in the cellar with the waxwork, and said nothing about it."

"They'd have had to bury Allsop too."

"If you hadn't been there, and Allsop hadn't been told about the buttons, he mightn't have gone into the music room at all. He mightn't have seen the body if he had gone in — somebody would have got in there first and covered it up."

"Roberts? And how about Miss Elena Clayborn?"

"Roberts — I'm leaving him out of this, there isn't a thing on his mind but shock — Roberts wouldn't have known a thing about the Fitch body. They'd have told him never mind, they'd get rid of the wax figure in the cellar. They'd have told Mrs. Leeder and the girl the same. They'd have managed it somehow, those five; think they'd stick at it? Pass by a chance to avoid all this trouble and publicity? Think they'd rather have a murder case in the family, about somebody like Fitch who was killed twenty years ago?"

"I don't know what they would have done."

"I bet those five wouldn't have hesitated. Not Garth Clayborn — the way he impresses me. He wasn't in on the Fitch murder, but he's tough. What I'm wondering is, what kind of a person could live in the house all this time and know there was a dead woman up there, and stay sane waiting for her to be found? I don't think anybody could stand it and stay sane. If it wasn't Leeder, there's a brain here with a kink in it.

"Now we'll have Mrs. Leeder down, but first I'd like to know why she thought somebody was going to steal those buttons. It isn't the kind of thing a lady usually gets into her head about her family."

"That's the question you wanted to ask me, is it?"

"That and another. Why didn't these people make more of a row about your coming today? Not because you told them a story involving a coral necklace."

"One answer will do for both questions; but I'd prefer to have you get the answer from Mrs. Leeder."

"What makes you think she'll tell me?"

"She's not a fool; she knows that all kinds of things have to come out in a murder case."

Nordhall got up, went to the door, and spoke to someone in the hall. Then he came back and wrapped the wax head in the newspapers. He tossed the bundle to the window seat, where Gamadge was now kneeling on one knee and looking out at the dusky garden. A servants' wing projected to the right, cutting off any view of the premises on that side of the house.

Nordhall, standing at the table, said: "We'll never solve this case. People like these don't give one another away."

A police sergeant came to the door, stood aside, allowed Mrs. Leeder to pass him, and waited.

"All right, Crowley," said Nordhall. "No notes on this."

The sergeant withdrew; Mrs. Leeder remained where she was, pale and quiet as a ghost. She was wearing a short black dress in which she looked less tall and less mature than she had looked the day before. She asked: "Don't you always take everything down, Lieutenant Nordhall?"

"Not always. This is going to be off the record, Mrs. Leeder. If we can't use your information I'll forget it." He came forward and turned a comfortable chair so that she could face him in it when he sat down. "Just relax," he said. "You're only going to help us clear things up a little."

But she stayed as she was, looking at him. After a moment she said: "Rowe Leeder's name got into the papers once — by accident. It ruined his life and mine."

"You don't want to blame the Department for that, Mrs. Leeder. You can trust me, and you can trust Mr. Gamadge."

She turned her head slowly to address Gamadge: "I don't — I really don't know how you can ever forgive me for dragging you into this."

"I don't matter."

She sat down, Nordhall sat down, and Gamadge settled on the window seat.

"Now first of all, " said Nordhall, his arms on the table, his manner friendly and informal, "I want to know — just between ourselves, if it has nothing to do with the case — why you thought one of your family might be fixing it to steal buttons out of that sealed room."

"Hasn't Mr. Gamadge told you that?"

"No, he left it up to you."

"Other things were stolen from the house — things of value."

"Don't say. When?"

"Within the last ten years. The last thing — there were only three — went a few years ago."

"What things?"

"A Chinese seal, a tea-pot, and a mandarin robe."

Nordhall, looking at her steadily, tapped the fingers of one hand on the table. He asked: "Whose were they?"

"They were part of the estate. It wouldn't have done to tell anybody — tell Mr. Allsop. Even now —"

"He won't hear about it from me if it isn't necessary to tell him. I don't like these restrictive clauses in wills — they make a lot of trouble."

Mrs. Leeder said: "Oh, yes, you know about the will."

"I know about it, of course. All about it — how you had to keep that wax figure in the house with you. There's a lot of spite in wills like that. Well, I can see why the

133

family couldn't complain when you called in Mr. Gamadge."

"If they'd refused to let him come, I was ready to tell Mr. Allsop and risk it. But I must confess," said Mrs. Leeder, a bitter smile on her lips, "that I knew I shouldn't have to take that risk."

"You were afraid the same party that took the other things might have a try for those buttons?"

"Or for anything else of value that might be there. It seems very small of me now, doesn't it? It's hard to make people understand the strength of these feelings that develop among relatives. And we had to live together so much of the time."

Nordhall sat back and looked pensive. "I'd say there was a screw loose somewhere, Mrs. Leeder. Didn't that ever worry you?"

"You mean you think one of us was *mad?*"

"Or still is. They might have inherited it. Your grandmother, now: I don't care what the doctors say, they're too technical; a good many sensible people would say she was crazy or near it, fixing up that wax figure and having it sit there playing the piano; making arrangements so that you'd all have to keep it there until 1944."

"But all that developed in Grandmother after Nonie died."

"It did develop, though. This Nonie — was *she* all there — living like a dummy before there was a dummy? No life of her own?"

"Just a passive, weak-willed person, I supposed."

"What I'm getting at, there might be some mental weakness handed down, something that took a bad form and culminated in violence — the Fitch murder."

"I never saw any sign of it."

"Mr. Seward Clayborn — moody kind of individual."

"There are so many moody individuals, Lieutenant Nordhall."

"Well, if you can't help me along that line, you might be able to help me along another. I want you to think back to the day of your grandmother's funeral."

"Do you think" — she spoke as if in desperation — "do you really think I've been doing anything else since that room was opened?"

"That's good. I want you to tell me what everybody did and where they went when you all came back from the funeral."

"Mr. Allsop —"

"I know; he had a sort of combined statement ready for us when we came, poor old boy. But he wasn't here himself until that night after dinner when you sealed the room, and I'm glad to say we've decided to send him home."

"Thank Heaven. He was looking dreadful. He really was splendid, I never saw such control; but the thing nearly killed him."

"So I thought. Well, you all gave him something to give us, but what does it amount to? Nobody knows where anybody was that afternoon between five o'clock and dinnertime. Nobody saw anything. What I'd like is your individual recollection of that afternoon, and let's do it this way: questions and answers. Something might come out of it — you'd be surprised."

IX

THAT MUSTN'T BE

Nordhall stacked up his papers, placed the cardboard box on top of them, reached forward, and opened the Cribb solander. He passed it to Mrs. Leeder, who took a cigarette out of it without comment and mechanically.

Nordhall lighted it for her, and one for himself.

"Now, I know how hard all this must be on you, Mrs. Leeder," he said, "but I know the kind of sport you are. When you made up your mind that you weren't going to have any more valuable property snatched from under your nose, you acted like a sport — you weren't too scared of these people to send for Mr. Gamadge. Has he told you he was afraid he mightn't be let in to-day?"

"No." She turned her face towards Gamadge, and frowned a little. "I haven't seen him to talk to since he came."

"He's a man of experience, and the situation scared *him*. But he knew you were all set for opposition, so he followed your injunction and didn't speak to me or to his lawyer. Of course he was prepared to find the Fitch woman's body in the sealed room."

"That never entered my mind. Perhaps I was stupid, but it's hard to imagine —"

"It is. Well, as I was saying: some women would be shut up in their room by now, doctor sent for, aspirin out, somebody fanning them."

"Nobody is fanning my Aunt Cynthia."

"No; but Mr. Seward Clayborn is lying down on his bed, and his daughter won't allow the police to ask him any more questions till he's got over his headache."

"Seward has nervous headaches very often."

"What I mean is, you evidently don't have them. You have a lot of mental stamina. I won't pretend that there isn't going to be anything unpleasant for you in the quiz we're going to have; but you'll understand that the unpleasantness has got to be there. First of all, I want to explain to you why we're pretty sure that there's a smart, callous, cold-blooded murderer in this house right now. Somebody didn't just stroll in that afternoon twenty years ago and kill the Fitch woman for what she had on her or to keep her mouth shut; the Nagles, or any other friends of hers, are about as thin a proposition as could be.

"The murderer's here in this house; and we

138

mustn't go wrong about who it is."

"No," said Mrs. Leeder. "That mustn't be."

"You're determined to prevent it if you can, I see that much. Well: about our evidence. In the first place" — he picked up the Cribb solander and held it in front of her — "doesn't this thing belong upstairs?"

"Yes, I think it does." She looked surprised. "There are several."

"How many?"

"This, and one in the reception-room, and one that I think was usually kept down here."

Nordhall showed her *A Season in the Cotswolds*. "This?"

"Yes. There was another that we had in the sitting-room, somebody's poems. It wore out or fell to pieces."

"But this was, as a usual thing, in the sitting-room — this Cribb?"

"Yes, it's a good colour for the sitting-room."

"How did you and Mr. Seward Clayborn pick them, Mrs. Leeder? I mean who decided that they'd make good cigarette boxes, and wouldn't be missed as books?"

"There were a lot of books of Grandfather's that had something wrong with them, but nice bindings. Seward had seen these cigarette boxes in some decorator's shop, and he asked

Uncle Gavan whether he and I couldn't make solanders out of those imperfect books."

"What was wrong with the books?"

She thought. "The Dante — there was only one volume out of three. Nobody knew what had become of the other volumes; but Grandfather liked auctions, and we thought he had picked up an odd lot of books, just for the fun of seeing what would turn up among them when they were unpacked." She looked at Gamadge. "Don't people often do that?"

"Yes," he said. "It's great fun. Sometimes it's a box of letters or papers — you buy them as 'sight unseen' and look for rarities. You don't as a rule find any."

"What about this walk in the Cotswolds?" asked Nordhall.

"Season," suggested Gamadge. "The titled authoress spent a summer there, presumably."

"Uncle Gavan said it must have been printed by her relations," said Mrs. Leeder. "And the coloured plates had been torn out."

"And the Cribb journal?"

"Mr. Gamadge seemed to think it ought to have been kept." She looked at Gamadge again. "Didn't you? What *did* you say — about sugar and pickaxes?"

"Sugar and pickaxes?" asked Nordhall.

"That Thug ritual I was telling you about," said Gamadge.

"Oh, yes. Why was this book used as a box, Mrs. Leeder?"

"There were pages missing or something. Is all this important, Lieutenant Nordhall? But I suppose it must be or you wouldn't ask the questions."

"I'd like to know who finally decided to convert this book into a box — who read it to see why it needn't be kept as a book; who could have read it."

"Any of us could have read it, I suppose."

"Who'd be likely to?"

"I don't know. Anybody reads anything, I suppose, if there's nothing better on hand."

"Mr. Leeder read the books here in this house?"

Nordhall's questions, coming fast and along lines he had not prepared her for, had had the effect he wanted of hurrying and perplexing her. But at this one she stopped, collected herself, and looked at him coldly. She said: "He never cared much for reading."

"But he may have sat around here reading — on a rainy day?"

"Yes, he may."

"I'm interested in this Cribb thing because Mr. Gamadge found it hidden here."

"Hidden?" She looked astonished.

"Among the other books, as if it *was* a book. Does anybody in the house do much reading

141

in these books down here?"

"I don't think so. They're the kind that everybody is supposed to read and hardly anybody does."

Gamadge cast a mournful look at a large-paper edition of Balzac in the case nearest him.

"Then this Cribb thing would have been as good as lost for a day or two?" asked Nordhall.

"I don't think anybody would have noticed that it had gone — for a day or two. Then Roberts would have looked around the house for it."

"It was in the sitting-room yesterday. Nobody knew Mr. Gamadge was coming here, did they?"

"No." She looked at Gamadge. "Not even Ena. It was through her that Mr. Gamadge came, but she didn't know it. I hope he wasn't too much annoyed with me when he found out that Mr. Malcolm —"

"Mr. Gamadge isn't annoyed. All these people, including Mr. Leeder, knew that Mr. Gamadge was interested in books, knew about old books?"

"Yes, I think so. Lieutenant Nordhall, what *is* it about this Cribb thing?"

"I'll tell you, and it's something I haven't even told Mr. Gamadge yet."

Nordhall sat up, drew the cardboard box

nearer to him, lifted the cover, and slowly produced from within a few inches of what looked like silk cord. It was yellow, tarnished to old gold; and from its frayed end there protruded two tiny strands of wire.

Mrs. Leeder said blankly: "That's our lamp cord."

"Yes, and Roberts told me all about it. It was put in when the house was converted to electricity, nearly fifty years ago. The electricians left so much of an extra supply that no flex has ever had to be bought since. This kind couldn't be bought now. The coils of it have always been kept in a drawer of a cupboard in the studio, where other house supplies were kept — picture wire and picture hooks, paper and string, screw eyes and such things. You know that drawer, Mrs. Leeder?"

"Of course."

"But outsiders wouldn't be likely to know it, would they? People like the Nagles?"

"I shouldn't think so."

"Mr. Leeder, though — he'd lived in the house two years after you were married. You couldn't call him an outsider."

"Why should — what do you mean about it?"

"This length was what the Fitch woman was strangled with."

Mrs. Leeder gave a faint cry, and her hands

closed on the arms of her chair.

"I wouldn't show it to you," said Nordhall, "if it wasn't necessary. I wouldn't talk about it if I didn't have to. But this is the neatest, quickest, quietest, surest method of murder there is, Mrs. Leeder — takes only a few seconds. The victim's breath is choked off right away, choked off for good; after the ends are pulled tight you couldn't get a finger in. Why isn't it a method that's used all the time, then? Well, I don't have to say."

Mrs. Leeder sat dumbly, her eyes on the end of yellow cord.

"It isn't always used," continued Nordhall, "because of course the murderer has to get up behind the victim first. That can't always be arranged. And when it is used, the murder is premeditated. Take this case: nobody found a coil of house wire loose, grabbed it up, and killed Fitch with it on the spur of the moment.

"We can draw several conclusions from this wire, then: The murderer knew that there was lots of the stuff, in handy lengths, in the studio cupboard: therefore, the murderer knew this house pretty well; therefore, the Nagles are probably out — and so is anybody else that didn't live here.

"I draw another conclusion: that the murder wasn't committed in the music room, but in the studio. Here's the picture: This Fitch woman found somebody in the music room, somebody who had got hold of the key after you all came back from the funeral that afternoon. Well, imagine your uncle or aunt, or your cousin Seward, or Leeder, caught by the Fitch woman stealing buttons. Very bad position. Unbearable.

"But that person couldn't very well go to the studio and get a length of wire out of the drawer and come back and strangle Fitch with it. Fitch wouldn't have waited in there with her back turned. But if she went into the studio to talk things over with this party, the party could have grabbed a chance.

"Then the little Fitch woman was dragged back into the music room and put on the sofa in the corner and locked in; and the key was returned to wherever Mr. Gavan Clayborn kept it. The door wasn't going to be opened again — would an outsider know that?"

Mrs. Leeder said clearly: "Rowe Leeder had gone. He wouldn't have known anything about it."

"Perhaps not. He'd only been gone a week or so; perhaps he had contacts in the house still. Anyway, Fitch's handbag was taken. Perhaps there was a receipt in it that told the murderer where to find her luggage. Perhaps the luggage was claimed and taken somewhere else — hotel room, another checking office; never mind that. What I'd like to have you know is that one of the chapters in this Cribb book was about Indian thugs — they strangled people from behind."

Mrs. Leeder said almost inaudibly: "Absurd."

"Is it? Then why was the thing hidden after Mr. Gamadge came here yesterday? The murderer had a pretty good idea that it was safe to leave it around among the family — that *they* hadn't read it. But Gamadge, a book expert, shows up, and it's hidden. If it hadn't been hidden we couldn't do a thing with it at a trial, not a thing, but now it corroborates the plain fact that the murder was committed by an inmate of the house, or somebody who had been one."

"Only we'd have to find another copy of Sir Arthur Wilson Cribb's *Journals in the Punjaub*," said Gamadge.

Nordhall looked at him. "Trust you to think of that."

"Who wouldn't?"

"Can we find one?"

"I dare say one exists in the British Museum, anyhow."

"Would they let us have a transcription made?"

"I'm sure they would. They're all for eliminating murderers over there."

Nordhall turned back to Mrs. Leeder. "Well," he said, "there you have it, as far as I've got it myself. You can see whether or not I'm hoping for a little light on the subject from you, Mrs. Leeder. Anything at all that would help me. Anything," he went on, while Gamadge regarded him with a certain admiration, "that you can remember about that afternoon twenty years ago."

She said: "I told it all to Mr. Allsop."

"Tell it all to me. It's easy to get off on the wrong track in a case of this kind; I wouldn't want to do that — waste time. You wouldn't want me to do it. But what's the logical thing to do, if there isn't any other lead at all? The logical thing is to get after the man or woman in the case with a bad record."

She said: "I knew it. I knew it."

"Of course you knew it; everybody knows it. Leeder was involved in another murder case."

"That's so unfair. So unfair. You oughtn't to bring that into it at all. My husband — Rowe Leeder had an alibi."

"Yes. Three people said he was somewhere else. They didn't even get as far as swearing it, they just said so. You'd be surprised, Mrs. Leeder, how many known murderers have got off scot free because three people — half a dozen people — swore on the Bible that they were somewhere else."

"Yes — gangsters."

"People that didn't want to see justice done."

"You simply can't involve Rowe in this after that alibi."

"I'll tell you when we can't use evidence against a man, Mrs. Leeder — when he's been tried for a crime and acquitted. That's when. Perhaps you acquitted him; anyway, you let him come back here ten years later. Why? Because you knew he hadn't been a particular friend of the Sillerman girl's, but only a client? A drug client?"

She laughed. "Drugs! Rowe Leeder!"

"I was just trying to understand why you let him come back. Plenty of women will forgive murder, forgive anything, before they forgive a man for running after another woman — a man they've only been married to for two years."

If Nordhall's easy way of dealing with pronouns seemed to introduce a note of polygamy into the subject under discussion, it at least conveyed his meaning to Mrs. Leeder. She said: "Women let men come back because they want to see them."

"Yes," agreed Nordhall, "but then they usually remarry."

"Rowe wouldn't have considered it. It would have revived the old scandal, and that's the last thing he wanted. He protected us from it in every way; outsiders didn't know he came here. Roberts understood that if other callers came he must warn Rowe before bringing them up to the sitting-room."

"And then Leeder would hide?"

"No, certainly not. He would go out the back way, by the alley."

"It looks to me as if Leeder had good reasons of his own for pushing in again like that. But you say definitely that so far as you know he wasn't here the day of your grandmother's funeral?"

"He wasn't even at the funeral."

"Had he kept his latchkeys to this house?"

"I don't know. He never used a latchkey after he began to come back."

Nordhall shuffled papers. "Your grandmother died November 6, 1924. The funeral was on the 10th. Where?"

"St. Thomas's chapel."

"Who went from this house?"

"All of us. Uncle Gavan and Aunt Cynthia, Seward and his wife, my father and mother and I, Roberts and Aggie Fitch and some of the maids."

"Mr. Allsop has a note here that you only went because your parents thought it would be best. You would have liked to stay home on account of this horrible scandal about Leeder."

"Yes. Not because of the scandal, but because he'd left. I wasn't in a state of mind to go anywhere."

"But your mother thought it would cause more talk if you didn't go. There was a five-year-old child in the house — Garth Clayborn. What happened to him?"

"Mother had taken him down to a day nursery she was interested in and left him there in the charge of the superintendent."

"Miss Fitch wore a red hat and a red dress to the funeral."

"Yes. Grandmother didn't approve of mourning, but the Clayborns did. We all wore the usual black, and crêpe veils."

"Leeder might have been in the back of the chapel somewhere?"

She said wearily: "You don't understand, Lieutenant Nordhall. He had disappeared. He was still in the papers, but the reporters couldn't find him. Nobody could. He wouldn't have come to a funeral."

"Well, then. You all drove up to Woodlawn, Miss Fitch still with you."

"She went in a car with Roberts and Grandmother's maid. The maid didn't come back to the house; as you probably know, none of the servants except Roberts came back at all."

"What time did you get back?"

"About five."

"Roberts says he was downstairs getting tea, and he brought it up to the sitting-room. Then he was busy getting supper for you all, and never came upstairs again that afternoon except to take the tray down again."

"Yes. He was very busy."

"What did you do?"

"I came in with Mother, and I saw Aggie Fitch go past us upstairs. I never saw her again. Mother only came in for a minute, to take off her veil. She took it off in the downstairs hall, and then went back downtown to get Garth. I went up to the sitting-room and waited for her and had tea."

"Garth's nursery was on the top floor, the suite Mr. Seward Clayborn and his daughter have now?"

"Yes."

"You didn't see any comings or goings at all?"

"No; after tea I went to my bedroom in the east wing."

"Your mother took Garth up to his nursery; when?"

"Before six, I think. She wasn't gone very long. He had his supper before six, always."

"We'll never know what she saw up on that top floor, if she saw anything. Mr. Clayborn's room was there, the room Garth has now; but he says he didn't go up. He stayed in the library, going over estate papers. Garth doesn't even remember being taken to a day nursery — doesn't remember a thing."

Mrs. Leeder asked: "You already knew about the day nursery?"

"Of course," said Nordhall, surprised. "Miss Clayborn has given me her statement."

Mrs. Leeder leaned her head against the back of her chair. She was beginning to be exhausted by this formidable policeman.

"Well, it sounds funny to me," said Nordhall. "Any way you look at it it's funny. You all assumed that Fitch was going, nobody went to find her and see if she was getting off all right, nobody wondered why she hadn't said good-bye to anyone."

"It was like Aggie to behave in that way — slip off. And we had our own affairs to think of."

"Only she didn't slip off; she was up there dead in the locked room all the time. She was never listed as missing; if her luggage was left somewhere unclaimed, without any means of identification in it, it would be opened after a lapse of time and auctioned off. Her identifying papers were in her handbag, and that went with the murderer."

Mrs. Leeder said: "I suppose it would be silly of me to remind you —"

"Go right ahead, I'll be glad to be reminded of anything."

"Roberts was so busy that day, and the back door may have been unlocked while he was in the kitchen. Aggie Fitch may have known all kinds of queer people; she may have told them all about us and our plans, and all about the house. There's no way of knowing that they hadn't been into the cupboards in the studio. There's no way of knowing that they hadn't seen the lamp wire."

"Did they hide this Cribb box yesterday? Or to-day?"

As she did not answer, he rose. She got up too.

"Let me remind *you* of something," he said gravely. "We may never solve this murder. You'll all be clearing out of this house pretty soon, and some of you may be living together somewhere else. Don't forget that one of the circle doesn't stick at homicide, and may be a case for the psychiatrists. Mrs. Leeder, don't hold out on me."

She said: "I haven't."

"All right for now, then."

When she had gone, Nordhall slowly let out a breath. He said: "Unless she knows something about Leeder, she doesn't know a thing. She'd throw the rest of them out of the window if she could save him that way."

Gamadge had picked up the Cribb solander and was turning it in his hands. He said: "I think she would."

Sergeant Crowley looked in. "Some people are here, name of Nagle."

"Where did you put them?"

"In the parlour."

"Wait till I get upstairs, then bring 'em up. No use telling my story twice again."

X

GARTH

Nordhall wrapped the head of Nonie tightly up in its newspapers and stood looking around the library. He said: "Don't suppose the Clayborns want this souvenir, but neither do I." He went over to a black-oak cabinet, opened it, and stuffed the parcel in on top of some old atlases. Then he came back, picked up his papers and the cardboard box, and said: "Let's go."

The big hall was empty, silent, and dimly lighted, the light filtering through coloured glass globes upheld by a bronze figure on the newel post. As Nordhall and Gamadge reached the foot of the stairs, a face with the reddish-purple glow of the lamps on it leaned over the balustrade just at the turn of the landing.

"Lieutenant Nordhall . . ."

"Yes?"

Garth Clayborn came farther down the flight, his hand on the rail. He said: "Would there be any objection if I got out of this place for a breath of air?"

Nordhall stood looking up at him. He said: "None that I know of, if you can keep clear of the Press. I don't want you talking to newspapermen and getting your picture taken. Not yet."

"I can keep clear of them. It's the best thing I do," said Garth, laughing, "keeping clear of people I don't want to see. I've had plenty of practice."

"Bet you have." Nordhall studied him. "But these fellers — once they get you backed up against a wall, you talk before you know you're talking."

"I'll go out the back way."

Nordhall asked: "Did you think *they* hadn't found the back way? We have two men out there, just to start with."

"I'll get by."

"Would you just as soon wait until a little later, Mr. Clayborn? I have some evidence to put before the family, and you're a member of it and one of the heirs of the estate. You ought to hear what I have to say."

"All right." Garth's furtive, amused face showed curiosity. "What kind of evidence?"

"You'll know right away if you'll go up to the sitting-room with the rest of them." Nordhall waited a moment, and then asked: "Where did you think of going to?"

"I thought I'd have a walk and a bite of

supper somewhere. I wouldn't look up any of my friends or go to my club. I wouldn't drop in anywhere I'm known." Garth added, his narrow face serious: "This thing gets on your nerves."

"It would on mine, in your place."

"First I didn't quite take it in; too pulpy," said Garth, coming down the stairs until he stood beside Nordhall. "Now I'm beginning to see how it'll look in the papers, with those pictures they take. I'd like to get out of this morgue for an hour or so and forget about it. After all, it does happen to be my birthday."

"It's hard on you two young people, mighty tough. Does Miss Elena Clayborn want to go out too?"

"She's worrying about her father. But I — nobody in the place cares anything about me, except perhaps Uncle Van; and he only cares because I'm the only Clayborn that can hand down the name. So why should I bother about them?"

"No reason. Too bad you were home at all; you might as well be somewhere else," said Nordhall, "for all you can tell us about the Fitch killing." He added: "Or about anything else."

Garth smiled. "I could tell you one thing."

"You could, could you?"

"Yes. I could tell you —"

"Here?" Nordhall glanced about him.

"Safest place in the house. Do you think anything I say can be heard in the room down here, or anywhere else in this cathedral?"

"Probably not."

"Absolutely not." But Garth lowered his voice. "I could tell you why Leeder came back."

Nordhall, interested, looked at him. "You mean ten years ago? The first time he came back here after the Sillerman scandal?"

"I didn't put the date in my line-a-day book, and I don't know that he hadn't been back before. He could have prowled around any night, any time; this is a quiet house to move around in," said Garth, smiling, "especially if you use the alley and the back door."

Nordhall, smiling benevolently in return, said he supposed it was.

"But whenever Leeder did come back, he came back to spy."

"That so?"

"I was a kid at school; my room was the same as it is now — next to that death cell on the top floor. How would you like to remember that, if you were me?"

"Tough."

"I'd come hustling upstairs after school, or

I'd be in my room and happen to look out through a crack in the door."

Nordhall said, amused: "When I look out through a crack in a door I don't happen to; I do it on purpose."

"I mean I'd get a glimpse before the door was entirely open," said Garth. "There Leeder would be, more than once or twice, wandering around or feeling of the sealed door with his thumb."

"Feeling of it?"

"Feeling around the moulding, as if he wanted to be sure it really was sealed. He wasn't here when they did it, you know; he'd been thrown out by my great-grandmother."

"Who'd he hear of it from?"

"Harriet, of course, " said Garth impatiently. "I didn't see him at it before the time he came back openly. If he did ever come back before, I was probably asleep in bed. Once or twice, after I'd seen him up there, I made it my business to find out that he was supposed to have left the house. Wouldn't it make you sick," inquired Garth with sudden low intensity, "to think he's getting a sixth of the estate?"

"By accident, too," said Nordhall, shaking his head gloomily.

"Of course by accident. I don't suppose he absolutely knew Great-grandmother Clayborn would have the stroke. Harriet's going to leave all her money to him, or she will unless she changes her mind now. But I can tell you one thing — whatever he gets won't last long. If there's a horse running he'll have something on the race. You can't win at that game," said Garth, with feeling. "Nix. Certainly not these days, and not any days if you don't stop betting."

"And who wants to stop?" asked Nordhall.

Garth looked at him shrewdly for a moment, looked at Gamadge, and said: "Perhaps you'll think I've let that business —" he glanced upward into the shadows — "let it get on my nerves —"

"I don't see a sign of it," Nordhall assured him.

"I mean you may think so when I've told you what I did a little while ago. It just occurred to me that if any Clayborn died intestate, the less Clayborns there were the more money there'd be to divide up. And Harriet might not change her will even now. So, rather than let Rowe Leeder cut in on anything more — anything of mine — half an hour ago I made *my* will. Just a temporary one, you know, but you bet it's legal, I had Allsop and Roberts witness it."

"Well," said Nordhall, eyeing him, "it's always a good thing to make a will."

"So I thought. Allsop will keep mine until

I get a chance to make a more formal one, and he'll spread the news. Perhaps Uncle Van and Aunt Cynthia will take the hint; as it is now, they'll just have left their property back to the family. Seward's, of course, goes to Ena; and I'm not sure . . ." Garth paused, and then said: "I'm not sure he'd worry anyway."

Nordhall digested this. Then he added: "Would it be all right for me to inquire who you're leaving your money to, Mr. Clayborn?"

At this Garth snickered aloud. "You wouldn't guess."

"Ought I to?"

"It's rich. You ought to have seen Allsop's face. They can't say a word — none of them."

"Why not?"

"Because I left all I died possessed of to the Clayborn Quartette."

At this Nordhall had to smile too. He said: "That was nice of you."

"It's only temporary, you know."

"Well, I'm much obliged to you for the information. Now will you just come up and listen to what I have to tell the family? Not that you seem to need telling much. And the Nagles — they'll want to see all the Clayborns," said Nordhall, with a ghostly smile. "I certainly would in their place. I think I'd insist on it."

"O Lord, are they here? The family says they're the perishing limit."

"They think they're the family too."

"And this gives them a look-in, does it?"

"They think so. Now just go on up, Mr. Clayborn; I'll be with you in a minute."

Garth mounted to the second floor. Nordhall looked after him, and then reflectively at Gamadge.

"Oh, yes," said Gamadge. "He's up to something."

"Putting it on Leeder, with a side bet on Seward?"

"I didn't mean that. It's this airing he wants to take; didn't you see the look in his eye?"

"You're dreaming. Who'd want *him* as an accessory after the fact?"

"Mrs. Leeder says he's a snooper."

"Well, follow him up if you want to," said Nordhall. "A private car will tail him better than a police car; but I think you're dreaming. He's just got some girl."

Gamadge stood where he was until Nordhall had disappeared; then he went slowly along to the door of the back passage, opened it, went through, and closed it behind him. He picked up the telephone and dialled.

He waited for a reply with both elbows on the shelf, tenseness in his attitude, and a frown upon his brow that altered his face astonishingly; for it was not entirely a frown of concentration.

Malcolm answered. "For Heaven's sake," he complained, "do you know it's nearly four hours that I've been sitting at home waiting to hear from you?"

"That's nothing. You're a detective. The police have wished a job on us — not very urgently, I must confess — but I'm taking them at their word."

"The police? What on earth —"

"Tell you when I see you, of course not now. Where's your car?"

"In the garage."

"Go and get it, or mine, whichever is handiest. Drive right up here to where I am, but approach by the rear."

"The rear?"

"Next street; there's an alley. The young gentleman who's a great favourite of yours — the one who thinks you're a little black man, the one whose name begins with a G —"

"Go on and make it perfectly clear, won't you? I might not quite understand whom you mean."

"In a short time he'll come out of the alley and go somewhere — doubtless by cab. Follow him, and don't lose him until he comes home. Then telephone instantly to me."

"The dinner hour approaches."

"We'll have something to eat somewhere afterwards."

"Suppose he stays out all night?"

"Then you can stay out all night."

"Or telephone you if I can?"

"If you can without losing him."

"I never trailed anybody before, dare say I can do it. Can't you give me some idea of what's been going on up there?"

"No idea, and only one descriptive word. The word is eldritch."

"Is what?"

"Eldritch. Now get going."

Gamadge replaced the telephone, and for a short time stood looking at it. Then he walked along the passage to a farther door, opened it, and went through into a kitchen hallway and a lobby beyond. He unlocked a back door and pulled it towards him.

The big garden was dark, but he made out shrubs, walks and trees. Past the far wall he could make out a low house, and at a gate in the wall he saw the large form of a man. There would be another in the alley, he supposed; Nordhall's mercenaries.

He came back to the main hall and went upstairs.

XI

MOURNERS

When Gamadge entered the sitting-room he found that Nordhall had taken up a commanding position in front of the fire. The cardboard box was on the mantel shelf; its cover was half off, and the end of yellow flex protruded from it like the head of a small fanged serpent.

Facing him, across the empty space where the tea table had been yesterday, three chairs were now drawn up. They were occupied by a bald man, a nervous-looking woman, and a lank girl. Mrs. Leeder was in her usual place on the sofa at Nordhall's right, her uncle and aunt sat opposite her, Mr. Allsop hovered behind them, and Seward and Elena were side by side on the nearest window seat. Garth occupied the one at the end of the room. Leeder stood leaning against the wall to the right of the doorway.

When Gamadge came in Mrs. Leeder held up her hand, a gesture of invitation. He passed the lank girl — rather an oldish girl, he saw, when he got a look at her — and sat beside his client. As there seemed to be a lull in the proceedings, he looked at the Nagles.

Nagle was a battered-looking little man, the battered look being partly due to the facts that his brown suit needed pressing, his brown shoes polishing, his brown felt hat blocking and cleaning; some people would have said that the hat needed throwing away. He had round bright eyes and a thin, satirical mouth.

His wife was pale haired and pale eyed, in new autumn clothes; a purple suit, and a purple hat which was tilted forward at such an improbable angle that Gamadge was sure Miss Nagle had given it a final twitch before they left home, with an injunction to keep it that way. Mrs. Nagle kept putting a gloved hand up to the brim, and then taking the hand away again. Gamadge imagined that she resembled the deceased Aggie Fitch.

The daughter was highly groomed and fashionable, or rather she was like a sort of carbon copy of a fashionable young woman; a copy of inferior materials and finish. Or perhaps, Gamadge thought, it would be more accurate to call her a faintly caricatured rough draft of a model. Her skin, pale as Mrs. Leeder's, was not clear; her eyes incessantly wandered; she was slumped down in her chair, with her long feet in their crippling shoes stretched out and crossed in front of her; and her long, bony hands fidgeted with the enormous red bag in her lap. She looked excited.

Nordhall said: "Well, now you all know how Miss Fitch was killed, what she was killed with, and approximately when it must have happened. But none of you can help me out about it. As for Mr. Allsop, he definitely wasn't in the house until after dinner that evening; Mr. and Mrs. Nagle weren't here at all."

"We hadn't been here since a good while before Mrs. Clayborn died," said Mrs. Nagle, in a hurrying sort of way. "But we made it a duty to go to her funeral. Pews weren't reserved for our side of the family, and no car was provided to take us to the cemetery. I would have gone in poor Aggie's car, only it was so full of servants. I remember so well poor Aggie saying that after poor Mrs. Clayborn died things were taken out of her hands."

"Out of Miss Fitch's hands?" asked Nordhall. Mr. Nagle sat looking straight in front of him, Miss Nagle turned her head and gave her mother a quelling stare.

"Yes, of course," said Mrs. Nagle.

Miss Cynthia Clayborn, upright in her corner next to the fire, was smoking; but her cigarette had burned to a stub, and ash was falling on the floor. She did not notice it. She was looking at nobody, and her harsh features were like stone. She said: "Aggie Fitch was my mother's employee, you know."

"A trusted *friend*," mumbled Mrs. Nagle.

"Well, anyway," said Nordhall, "you didn't come back to this house after the funeral?"

"No, we didn't. Aggie was leaving."

"We thought Aggie was leaving," said Mr. Nagle in a slightly bantering tone.

"The room had been locked that morning," continued Nordhall, "that night it was sealed. Everybody wanted it sealed."

"Of course we did," said Miss Clayborn. "So would anybody."

"You have any voice in the matter?" Nordhall glanced down at Mrs. Leeder.

She replied: "I had an opinion. I wanted it sealed. I was rather young to have a voice."

"Well, anyway, that night it was sealed. But it was locked that morning, after you all went in and had a look. What were you looking for?"

His eyes were on Gavan Clayborn, who answered shortly: "For anything we might decide we didn't want inaccessibly shut up for twenty years."

"Nobody have any chance at those buttons then?"

"Nobody had thought of the buttons then," said Miss Clayborn.

"But could they have been taken? I'm trying to get conclusive evidence that they were not."

"Place was as bright as day," said Clayborn. "I was there myself. I saw what was done, and I saw the others out and didn't stay behind."

"And then you locked up. But why did you lock up, Mr. Clayborn? That's what I'm getting at. Why lock up, if there was nothing to steal — so far as you knew — and nobody to try to steal anything?"

Clayborn said after a pause: "Damned if I know why, unless I thought of it as a first step in the sealing."

Miss Clayborn said: "If my brother hadn't, I should have asked him to."

"Because it was all fixed up for sealing, and you didn't want anybody going in and poking around?"

Looking at him steadily, she said: "Yes."

Nagle observed: "Poor old Aggie went in and poked around, after all, didn't she?"

Nobody answered him.

"Where did you keep the key of the room, Mr. Clayborn?" asked Nordhall.

"In the top left-hand drawer of my dresser. Where it's been ever since, until to-day. I mean when I took it out to-day I shouldn't have known it had ever been taken out before."

"Well, that night you sealed up. Who was it wanted the window bricked?" And as he got no reply, he went on: "Surely you remember, some of you, who suggested a big undertaking like that?"

Seward said in his tired voice: "I think I made the first suggestion about bricking the window. I made it when we talked about sealing the door."

"Because some child on the roof next door might break a pane?"

"One had been broken downstairs some time before, by children throwing a ball on their way home from the Park."

Miss Clayborn said: "I thought it was a splendid idea to brick up the window. Those artists next door — they might easily get up on the roof and throw a bottle."

"Well, that's that," said Nordhall. "I have a clear picture, only it doesn't include Mr. Leeder."

Everybody in the room, except Mrs. Leeder, looked at Leeder. The Nagles craned back to look. Leeder said: "No, I was out of the picture."

"Didn't attend the funeral?"

"No."

"Where were you living at that time?"

"Where I live now," said Leeder, smiling a little. "No reason to move. I was always entirely satisfied with my landlady."

"Well, go ahead and tell us where it is," said Nordhall impatiently.

"I should have told you if you'd asked me. You haven't asked me anything," said Leeder.

"And the family can't tell me anything. Is it such a secret?"

Nagle, greatly amused, turned to look at Leeder again. He asked: "Say, Rowe, what is this? You mean none of them know you live with us?"

"They never asked me, Bert."

Nagle turned back to address the room in general with a cackle of laughter: "Say, what do you know? What a guy. Here he's been living with us in Jersey City for twenty years, and nobody knew it. Only boarder we ever had. And my wife thought you knew it, all the Clayborns knew it, thought she was doing the family a favour."

"I did not," said Mrs. Nagle. "I thought I was doing Aggie a favour. She always liked Rowe Leeder."

"So did we like him," said Nagle. "I got him his job on the *Great White World*, and now he's sports editor. Well, boy! You certainly play 'em close up to your chest!"

Mrs. Leeder, utterly amazed, said nothing.

Miss Clayborn spoke in tones of blank astonishment: "You've been living with the Nagles all these years, Rowe Leeder?"

"All these years, Miss Cynthia."

She looked across at Mrs. Leeder. "Did you know, Harriet?"

"No, of course not, Aunt Cynthia. If he'd wanted to tell me where he lived he'd have told me. I don't ask questions."

"It happened in the most natural way in the world," said Leeder. "Aggie Fitch fixed it up for me."

They stared at him, all the Clayborns.

"I said good-bye to Aggie," he went on, "the day I — er — left. She suggested the Nagles. It seemed a good idea to me at the time, and I never changed my mind about it."

"And *we* certainly haven't had a chance to talk about it to the family," remarked Mrs. Nagle in her tone of repressed resentment.

"All right, Lou," said her husband. "Never mind that. Perfectly natural, as Rowe says — for him to take refuge with relations. Aggie knew we were looking for a paying guest."

"Well," said Nordhall, "no matter how it happened, Mr. Leeder certainly kept it dark. Now about Miss Fitch disappearing, and what you thought, Mr. Nagle."

"She certainly disappeared," replied Nagle. "We thought it was funny when we didn't hear from her, but there was this cruise she was always talking about. The whole works — Gibraltar, Suez, India, China and Japan. Home by way of Honolulu. She'd done a lot of travelling with old Mrs. Clayborn and the daughter, she had her trip all doped out; pile of folders and language books a foot high. We thought she was too busy getting off to let us hear from her."

Nagle was very glib. Nordhall asked: "The ship was picked out?"

"Not that we knew."

"If you'd known the ship, you might have tried to follow her up that direction. Many such cruises at that time, in a year?"

"Don't know a thing about it," said Nagle. "We do our cruising at the news-reels."

"You saw her to speak to after the funeral. She never said a word then about her plans?"

"We only saw her for a minute; she was getting into the car."

"Mrs. Nagle was her niece, her only relative except this young lady here —"

"And the Clayborns," said Nagle, smiling. "She didn't say good-bye to them, either."

"But she was only a distant cousin of theirs, a second cousin of old Mrs. Clayborn. You'd be the people she'd keep in touch with. How long did you wait before making any inquiries about her?"

"My wife called up in a couple of weeks. We didn't care to butt in sooner, house of mourning and everything."

"And when they told you here that she'd been gone since the day of the funeral, you just let it go?"

"We thought Aggie was on her cruise."

"No picture cards from her, no word from her afterwards, no news that she'd died, no communication from anybody about her property. Your wife spoke to her at the funeral, she'd just sent you a lodger; you saw her regularly; but you never went to Missing Persons about her in all those years, advertised, did a thing. Leeder never did a thing, though she'd been the means of getting him a home and a job."

Nagle said: "Make what you like of it, Cop. We're busy people out our way; Leeder was taxiing until he got other work, no money in his pockets, and he'd been brought up rich. Think *he* had time to worry about Aggie Fitch?"

Mrs. Nagle said suddenly, in a shrill voice: "I knew they'd think it was funny, Bert. I'm going to tell about the little fight."

Nagle sat back in his chair, crossed his legs, and looked up at the ceiling.

"I can't help it," said Mrs. Nagle. "It sounds funnier this way."

Miss Nagle's voice was heard for the first time. She had been glancing about the room, at Garth on his distant window seat, at Gamadge with curiosity. Now she said: "What can you do, Pop? Let her go ahead and hand it to them. What can you do?"

"That's right, Mrs. Nagle," said Nordhall. "Tell us about the little fight."

Mrs. Nagle committed an act of defiance by shoving her hat into a comfortable position on her head. "That was a mistake," she said, "about my talking to Aggie at the funeral; I just noticed that there weren't any cars left for any more of us after Aggie and the servants drove away. It was before, the day of Mrs. Clayborn's death, that she said that over the telephone — about things being taken out of her hands."

"Your husband thought it would sound better if you put the conversation later, at the funeral?" asked Nordhall.

"No, I just got it mixed; I didn't talk to Aggie at the funeral. We had this little fight over the telephone. That's why I didn't expect to hear from her again. Of course if she'd lived, it would have blown over."

"But you weren't surprised that it didn't seem to have blown over?"

"Aggie was touchy. There wasn't much to it, but . . . you know how those things are.

I couldn't speak first. When we called up and found she'd gone —" Mrs. Nagle looked around at the assembled company in some confusion — "were told she'd gone, we thought she wasn't going to make up."

"What started the fight, Mrs. Nagle?"

"My daughter wished to be a dancer. She was only eight, but you have to start early. Mrs. Clayborn was going to pay for the lessons, but she died. And the very day she died Aggie didn't waste a minute; she called up and told me the lessons were off."

"So you wouldn't go ahead and arrange for them?"

"Yes, and you can imagine the shock it was. Lorina was half sick crying. *We* couldn't afford lessons, and we knew what would happen. That's what did happen; Lorina works in an office."

"Too bad."

"Aggie could have lent her the money till she got started on her career; by what my husband and I could figure — she was the kind of person that never talks about her money — she must have had plenty saved. I let myself go," confessed Mrs. Nagle. "I burned up the telephone."

"And then called up two weeks later to try and get a line on her and apologize?"

"Yes, of course I did. But when they said

here that they didn't know where she was, what could we do?"

"And you have no idea where her savings were?"

"We never had any idea. My husband thinks now —" she hesitated, and then went on in a flat voice — "he thinks she had her money on her."

"When she was killed?"

"Yes, or some bank would have advertised or found us or something."

"Well, it's much better to be frank, Mrs. Nagle; now we get a better idea of your motives in acting the way you did about her."

Nagle, who had not changed his attitude, said: "Yep. You get the idea. Now you won't have to put the blame for the killing on nice people like the Clayborns. You can say Leeder or my wife or I came over here that afternoon, Aggie let us in, and we killed her for her money — to give Lorina dancing lessons."

"Well, she's still waiting for 'em," said Nordhall.

"That won't bother you; there was a fight, that's enough. Rowe Leeder's old trouble will be raked up, and the papers will have the three of us running a murder academy." Nagle suddenly brought his head down and looked at Gavan Clayborn, a dangerous look. He said: "We'll have some good stories about

177

some of you people to hand out ourselves."

After a long pause Gavan Clayborn sat up, felt with deliberation for his cigar case, got it out of his pocket, opened it, and offered it to Nagle. He said: "She died here, Mr. Nagle; this is where they'll place the responsibility for her death. But wherever the responsibility does lie, the Clayborns owe you something. Have a cigar."

Mr. Allsop, looking apprehensive, came a step forward; Nagle sat gazing at Clayborn, motionless.

"Have a cigar and let's talk it over," said Clayborn. "The Clayborns owe you consideration."

Nagle, his bright round eyes fixed on the other, slowly took a cigar. While he clipped and lighted it, Clayborn replaced the case and went on:

"Right. I won't offer you a drink now, because there's a buffet supper getting assembled downstairs, what Roberts can scramble together for us; salads, cold stuff, and anything you like in beverages from cocoa to whisky. I hoped you'd do us the pleasure of going down and having something. I rather hoped that, sad as the occasion is, it might be an occasion for our young people to get acquainted."

Miss Nagle, turning her head to look at

Garth again, caught his expression of outrage. She favoured Gamadge with a cynical and worldly smile. But Mrs. Nagle looked eager.

"To tell you the truth," continued Gavan, "I'm very glad to have an opportunity of meeting you all in this informal way. Mr. Allsop and Lieutenant Nordhall being with us needn't make it formal. It's all in the family. They understand as we do — terrible tragedy, but it happened a long time ago. We can discuss it frankly."

Nagle was listening intently. He said: "My wife had a kind of an idea that Aggie being in your employ at the time — we haven't gone into it yet, perhaps we won't need to; but Aggie Fitch's money, whatever she had in her bag anyway, was stolen out of this house; and if she'd been putting up curtains and fallen off the ladder —"

"Exactly," said Gavan. "Very frank, plain talk, just what we want. We'll have a consultation with Mr. Allsop, and we'll abide by what he says — unless you want to get a lawyer of your own in. But you probably know that he's impartial in these matters. As for the present, we are glad to bear all immediate expenses and take all the responsibility off your hands. Bury her in the family plot, of course; and see that there's room left and places marked for you and your wife and daughter. I hope

179

Mrs. Nagle will consult with my sister about funeral arrangements, when there is a funeral. That's in the hands of the police. But you and your wife and daughter are naturally the principals, we take our marching orders from you."

Nagle recrossed his legs; he did not take his round bright eyes from Gavan's blue ones. To him Gavan Clayborn represented such power and influence, so much worldly experience and wealth, that he no doubt believed Clayborn quite able to get his own family out of any jam.

"You'll be in on our conferences with the police," continued Clayborn, "and with the Commissioner; I happen to know him a little, he's coming up when he gets into town. They'll leave no stone unturned. But — twenty years ago; who's to tell what happened?"

Mrs. Nagle said: "I don't know what Mr. Nagle was thinking about — saying we'd tell stories to the papers. Family stories! Imagine us telling family stories to the —"

Leeder spoke lazily: "Sit tight, Louisa. Nagle and Lolo may choke *you* to death if you don't. The Clayborns won't be able to give you a nickel if you shake them down in front of the Law. Just forget you have anything to sell."

"We haven't anything to sell," protested Mrs. Nagle.

"Everybody has family gossip to sell, and Nagle damn near put his foot in it a minute ago. You'll make a big mistake if you do talk to the papers, or let Lorina have her picture taken. I know she's dying to do that."

Miss Nagle made an affectionate face at him.

"It's Old Home Week," said Leeder. "Make the most of it. Nagle, take your family down and have something to eat and drink and go home. They won't stop you. Nobody really thinks you had anything to do with Aggie's taking-off. Did you even know a thing about those buttons?"

Mrs. Nagle said: "I don't know what you all mean about buttons. I never heard anything about buttons."

Miss Nagle asked: "Were they jools?"

Nordhall spoke at last: "Go on down and get your supper. Just keep around so we can get in touch with you later — don't leave your vicinity, and don't talk."

The Nagles rose. Leeder said: "I'll go down with you."

"I will," said Elena. She came forward and took Miss Nagle's arm.

Miss Clayborn said sharply: "Garth!"

"Sorry." Garth came lounging from his window. "I have to go out."

XII

QUELQUES FLEURS

With the departure from the room of the Nagles and Leeder, Elena and Garth, a silence fell. Gavan broke it: "We'll have to make up a sum of money — the heirs will," he said in a tone of calm resignation.

Nordhall was grinning from ear to ear. He looked at Gamadge. His expression seemed to say that these people were so used to getting away with anything that even the presence of a policeman didn't embarrass them. But Gamadge was quite sure that Nordhall's methods — celebrated among his friends — of disarming the opponents by fraternization, had hypnotized even Gavan Clayborn. That gentleman, glancing at Nordhall, remarked: "You see what I mean."

"Fair enough," smiled Nordhall. "And right out in the open. No extortion, or anything like that."

Mr. Allsop, not hypnotized, said anxiously: "It's quite understood that no question of — er — compensation has arisen. There can be no reason why the Clayborns shouldn't give these family connections a present." He looked exhausted and shaken, but he was very game. "An income to the girl, say; for I'm afraid —" he smiled bleakly — "that in the professional sense her dancing days must be over."

"Lucky, perhaps, for a suffering public," said Seward, "that they never began."

"She'd swallow anything," said Miss Clayborn, "to get into the house. I know that type. We'll never be rid of her now."

"We shan't be in the house, Aunt Cynthia," said Mrs. Leeder.

"She'll follow us up. She'll drop in. What in Heaven's name got into Rowe Leeder's head to stay with them all these years? It's the most extraordinary thing. I can't get over it at all."

Allsop said: "Speaking without prejudice, I might say that perhaps he had his very good reasons for staying there."

"If he hadn't reasons," replied Miss Clayborn shortly, "he wouldn't have stayed."

"It's a combination," agreed Nordhall, "it's certainly a combination."

"Wouldn't trust the fellow — Nagle — farther than I could throw him," said Gavan.

"And after all these years," said Mr. Allsop, "as Mr. Leeder very pointedly remarked, it is probably doubtful that evidence will be found against anybody."

"It was Mr. Clayborn that pointedly remarked that," said Nordhall, laughing again.

"Whoever remarked it," said Allsop, "it is quite true. The question of fingerprints occurs to me; but everybody was in that music room on the day."

"I haven't given up all hope yet, Mr. Allsop," said Nordhall. "But I'm afraid you're right. That yellow cord doesn't take fingerprints, and Fitch's handbag's gone. Well: you all want me to pin it on the Nagles and Leeder."

Mrs. Leeder said: "No. Those Nagles looked like harmless people to me."

Nordhall looked down at her rather sternly. "You wouldn't call them a combination?" he asked. "From a professional's point of view the three of them make one, and a powerful one. I'll put it to you:

"They're living together, have been together since before the Fitch murder; and Leeder kept the fact a secret even from you.

"Money's the big motive for homicide, and they had no money; while all of you Clayborns had incomes and your livings paid for.

"Leeder knew all about the house and the family; and he could have got information about the proposed sealing of the music room from Fitch. After the murder, years afterwards, as soon as he decently could, he turned up here again to watch you all, to see whether the sealed room was tampered with, perhaps to — er — supply the combination with marketable loot. I'll just remark that Nagle looks like a crook, Mrs. Nagle's a cipher, the daughter's on the make; such people might have contacts with receivers of stolen goods, and Leeder once had dealings with the underworld.

"Figure it out without bias, Mrs. Leeder."

Miss Clayborn said faintly: "The awful, terrible part of it is that the Nagle woman looks like Aggie Fitch. I don't think I can face her again."

"No need for any of us to face her," growled her brother. "We'll have sandwiches and something to drink up here."

Mrs. Leeder rose. She said: "I'm going to my room. I don't want anything."

"You'd better have something, Harriet," said Miss Clayborn coldly.

"Just some coffee. I couldn't eat." She looked at Gamadge. "But you must go down and make some kind of meal, Mr. Gamadge — if you can bring yourself to swallow food in this house."

Nordhall said: "Food is food. Just come on upstairs with me first, Gamadge, will you?"

185

They went out of the sitting-room, and up to the top floor. A uniformed man was stationed in front of the music room, whose door stood ajar to allow the passage of a long, thick electric wire.

Nordhall addressed him: "All right, Mulvane. Go down and get yourself something to eat. Then take the front — let Goldstein go home."

The uniformed man departed, and Nordhall pushed open the door. Gamadge entered behind him.

The music room was now brightly lighted by a high-powered bulb fitted to an old standard lamp, and it was thoroughly ventilated; several bricks had been knocked away outside the open middle window-pane. Fresh cold air blew in through the gap; the evening had turned chilly, and there was a stiff breeze.

Gamadge stood and surveyed the place with some interest. It was bare, as a music room should be; without pictures on the silvery rough-plastered walls, without curtains or upholstery. The slate-blue floor was of some cork-like composition, the rug a plain silvery-blue.

Dominating the place, the open baby-grand piano stood in the south-east corner, where light from the windows had once fallen over the left shoulder of a player, to the keyboard.

The piano lid was propped up in concert style, and there were candles on the holders and a sheet of music on the rack; near by, a handsome old canterbury held other music. The piano stool, which swivelled on a screw, had a comfortable padded seat of velvet.

There was little other furniture. A small, lady's desk of carved maple, and a chair to match, stood against the north wall; an old-fashioned sewing table of mahogany, nearer the door on the same side, had a small armchair in front of it. The sofa on which the dead woman had lain, and on which Nonie had perhaps often reposed after her practising, had made up the list of furnishings sealed into the room twenty years before.

Gamadge walked over to the piano. The music on the rack was a Chopin prelude, and looked difficult to play.

Nordhall said: "We could take the whole thing to pieces."

Gamadge bent over and looked into the piano. He said: "I think you've got the wrong idea, Nordhall. If anything was hidden here, it wasn't to be hidden for ever. The old lady didn't mean that. If she laid a button-case on these wires she put it there to emphasize the fact that the buttons were to remain Nonie's property for the duration."

"Glad to take your word for it." Nordhall

followed him to the desk, and stood behind him when he sat down. "You can take my word for it that there isn't any secret compartment in that little thing; it's modern. And none in the sewing table."

Gamadge pulled down the lid, and began to finger the objects in the well; a fancy china inkpot and penholder, a penwiper shaped like a dahlia with flannel leaves. He said: "Where moths do not corrupt. This thing is like new."

"Look at all the two-cent stamps," murmured Nordhall in a nostalgic tone.

The two-cent stamps were in a china box. Gamadge pulled forth a box containing a jade-handled seal and some sticks of blue sealing wax. Then he shoved everything back again into the well, and began to empty the pigeon-holes.

"Nothing," said Nordhall.

"A life," said Gamadge. "Letters from women or girls asking her to lunch, or referring to charity board meetings or bridge teas. Dance cards kept for years, because the dances were all taken. I suppose Miss Winonah Clayborn would always have partners. A note from a man thanking her for the delightful theatre party and supper. She didn't keep much."

He attacked the contents of another pigeonhole.

"Bills," said Nordhall. "Look at the one for piano lessons for three months. The guy must have been a big shot. And, my God, don't miss the one for the piece of fancy work you'll see in the work-table. Just the canvas and wool — eighty-five dollars."

"*Unique Spanish Gros Point chair cover,*" read Gamadge. "*Flower centres worked in petit point.* Work of art, Nordhall."

"Guess they have to spend their money some way."

"Don't grudge her her fancy work; must have been very calming." He opened another bill. "This is from her florist; she gave a lunch party." He read: "*Twelve Corsage Bouquets, green orchid and spray, sixty dollars.*"

"Made a sweater for herself," said Nordhall, entering into the spirit of the thing: "*Twelve balls imported Shetland powder blue wool, nine balls white angora.*"

"Made herself some lingerie," said Gamadge. "*Five yards white nainsook, ten yards Irish lace edging.* And here are some cosmetics; she was very conservative. Orris root, lavender, Atkinson's Eau de Cologne."

"More perfumery," said Nordhall. "White Rose and Quelques Fleurs."

Gamadge said: "Rather dashing for Nonie." He looked at the bill. "Oh, that was a Christmas present she bought for somebody. Bill's dated December twenty-one, nineteen-one. Of course it was a Christmas present; she didn't use perfume — only Eau de Cologne. You don't get her at all."

"Then how about this?" asked Nordhall, offended. "Bought in April, nineteen-thirteen. Quelques Fleurs? That mean some flowers?"

"Yes."

"Then here's a thousand of 'em, five dollars a bottle."

Gamadge took the bill away from him and looked at it. He read: "*One half-dozen Mille-fleurs. Bandet & Co. Thirty dollars.* This isn't perfumery, Nordhall."

"It isn't?"

"It's buttons."

"You don't say so."

"They're painted with a lot of little flowers under glass. They're highly-esteemed by collectors; I looked buttons up yesterday after I got home. You'll find that Bandet was or is a dealer in antiques." He added: "The bill is dated the year before she died."

"Initial it, will you?" As Gamadge did so, Nordhall drew an envelope from his pocket, and carefully poured the contents upon a sheet of note paper from a pigeon-hole in the desk. The paper was edged and monogrammed in blue and silver, but Nordhall did not pause to admire it. He looked silently at Gamadge.

Gamadge bent his head to study the little heap of crushed glass and rainbow-coloured dust. He said: "That's one of them."

"It was this side of the piano, ground into the rug. Aggie Fitch came in, the other party swung around to face her and dropped a button and stepped on it. Picked up the metal backing, but couldn't pick up this." Nordhall poured the glinting heap back into the envelope, and put it and the bill for six mille-fleurs buttons into his wallet.

Gamadge glanced through the remaining papers, replaced them, and closed the desk.

"That's settled, then," continued Nordhall. "Party was stealing, was caught at it by Fitch, and Fitch was killed. Just one of those mean little thieveries rather than which some people would commit a worse crime than be found out." He added, as Gamadge got up and moved to the work-table: "Fitch's savings were just velvet."

"You don't care for the Leeder-Nagle combination so much now?" Gamadge sat down and lifted the mahogany lid.

"I care for any theory."

Gamadge inspected the contents of the little compartments in the top tray; old spools of silk and cotton, a gold thimble, small scissors with gilt handles, needle cases, a paper of fine English pins, bees-wax, a little emery bag, implements for sewing that Gamadge didn't know the uses of.

He pulled out the shallow drawer below. Knitting needles, hooks and eyes, buttons.

"No collectors' items here," he said, and pulled out the deep lower drawer. It overflowed with a big canvas square, many-coloured skeins of crewel wool; the blunt needle was still in the middle of a brilliant flower.

"That's the eighty-five dollar job," said Nordhall. "Perhaps one of the Clayborn ladies might like to finish it."

"Perhaps." Gamadge pushed the drawer in and stood up.

"Perhaps," continued Nordhall, looking about him, "that girls' school will go on having this for their music room."

"Foolish to waste it."

"I'll tell you one thing," said Nordhall, as they went out into the corridor, "if this hasn't been a haunted house yet, it never will be now."

"Leaving the light?" asked Gamadge.

"I was going to yank it out of the base-board along here, and throw the wire in and lock up; but why? We've finished in there, and if anything else is hidden it'll have to be sawed out. I guess you're right — nothing else is hidden."

Nordhall went back, turned out the light, and was coming through the doorway again when Mulvane called from the landing: "Somebody on the telephone for Mr. Gamadge."

Gamadge ran down to the lower floor, and into the telephone passage.

Malcolm was on the wire: "Boss, I lost him."

"Oh."

"But I have a story for you."

"Where are you now?"

"In a drugstore on Madison, around the corner from you."

"I'll join you; we'll eat somewhere. Just tell me first where he was heading when you gave up."

"Downtown."

"Oh. Well, I'll be with you in five minutes."

Gamadge quietly found his hat and coat, and let himself out into the vestibule. A policeman there took his name and told the assembled newsmen that this wasn't a Clayborn, and to give the feller a chance now.

Mr. Allsop had already run the gauntlet; Gamadge passed him at the corner, getting into a cab. The poor old gentleman looked very much bewildered still; he gave Gamadge a wild and questioning stare through the window as he was driven away.

Malcolm was standing in front of the drugstore beside the car; he did not look like an operative who had lost his subject, he looked rather pleased with himself.

"As the sorcerer's apprentice," he said, "I think I did pretty well without the password."

"I'll decide on that when I have your report. Are we following in Garth's footsteps?"

"Far as they go."

"Then we'll put the car in a garage — I know one three blocks east. We'll have supper in the only restaurant within a mile that serves food on Sunday. Walk there."

"What's the matter with riding?"

"I don't want Garth Clayborn noticing the car if he's had a glimpse of it already. Has he?"

"Might."

"Take no chances."

XIII

THE SPLENDID PLACE

Malcolm flatly refused to say a word until he had been told the story of the afternoon. It staggered him so completely that twice on their walk down to the restaurant — at the finding of Aggie Fitch, and at the fantasia of Sir Arthur Wilson Cribb and the yellow lamp wire — he stopped dead in his tracks. The second time he and Gamadge lost a light.

Gamadge was not pacified by his excuse that he was thinking of that poor kid Ena.

"Ena? Ena? She's irrelevant. Don't keep dragging your amours into this."

They had reached the restaurant that still fed people on Sundays, and there, amid the roar of voices, the clash of falling crockery, the shouts of waiters and the moan of the radio, Malcolm told his own tale:

"When Clayborn came out of the alley he never saw me; said something to the policeman there, and then made for Fifth Avenue and got a cab. The alley is between a big apartment and a little old rustic house. The old lady that

195

lives there thinks there's been a fire.

"I drove after him, and I don't know why there's so much fuss made about following people. It's as easy as falling off a log."

"You ought to know; you fell off."

"That was different. I mean I kept right after him to the upper Forties, and then across to Sixth Avenue. I thought of course that he was going through to some movie, but he wasn't. It's a dreary thoroughfare, isn't it?"

"You should have known it in its heyday, when the elevated was still running."

"It's bad enough now. I couldn't believe my eyes when he stopped the cab at the corner — the south-west corner. Nothing anywhere but dingy stores, all dark, and a run-down hotel."

The waiter brought cocktails, and then dashed away with their order.

Malcolm went on:

"He got out and paid the cab. I had the light with me, and thought it safest to drive across the avenue myself; but it wasn't too safe, as it happened. I nearly caught up with him. He was in front of an old four-storey building, brick, with a kind of round tower on the roof; what it can be for I don't know, shouldn't think it's meant for decoration. There's a cleaning and dyeing establishment on the ground floor, a tailor above, and I suppose flats in the two upper storeys. The third storey was lighted, the rest of the place dark. A sign in the tailor's window said *Spitano*.

"What was my astonishment when Garth walked a few yards along the street and went into the side entrance of the place. You must understand that the surroundings are squalid, and the building dingy and run-down. Here's the side street address."

Malcolm passed it over, and went on:

"I got out of the car and discreetly followed into a dark and filthy vestibule. There were bells and cards; only two. One said *Spitano*. One was illegible."

"Illegible?"

"The engraved name had been scored out. The inner door was unlocked, and I went into a narrow hall, very dirty, with no elevator and a flight of uncarpeted stairs. It was lighted only from above on some upper landing. By the way Garth Clayborn had gone into the place I knew he'd been there before.

"But he didn't stay long. I heard him coming down from the top floor, and I went back and got into the car, which I had left this side of a saloon. Unfortunately — and I don't know what I could have done about it — it's a west-bound street. If I'd stopped on the avenue I'd have lost sight of him."

"I understand."

"He came out again, thinking his own thoughts; and they were funny ones. He made for the corner, and he was in a southbound cab before I could back up and follow. I never laid eyes on him again, although I drove several blocks down. He turned off somewhere. He might have been making for some downtown hang-out. I thought I'd better make my report before I did any investigating of my own."

"You showed very good judgment. Wait here for me, I must telephone."

Gamadge found a booth, and called the Clayborn house. He asked for Nordhall.

Nordhall said: "You were a fool to go home; there's a spread here would make your mouth water."

"Malcolm followed Garth Clayborn, and now I'm going to investigate further. The trouble is, Malcolm lost him; he was headed downtown, but it's possible that he simply drove around the block and back to Fifth, and went back home. Will you find out if he did come back?"

"I'll find out; but why should I?"

"He's been poking into something that doesn't concern him; he might tackle somebody with his conclusions. He may not be safe in that house."

"I'd like a few details," said Nordhall, with interest.

"You'll get them all as soon as I have them, but meanwhile I want you to find out whether he came home. If he did, or when he does, I want an eye kept on him. Take no chances. There's a killer in the house, if I might remind you."

Nordhall was the last man in the world to underrate the importance of such a warning from that quarter. He said: "I get it," and asked: "When will you be back here?"

"As soon as I get that information. Lose no time now, for goodness' sake."

Gamadge went back to the table, where the short meal they had ordered was waiting. He and Malcolm swallowed it hastily, and then went out and got a cab.

They drove down Fifth Avenue, cleared now of its summer evening crowds and at its best; with its towers and steeples rising into the misty glow of the lower sky, and stars above. The trip was a short one, the journey across to Sixth very short. Gamadge paid the cab off on the east side of the way, and he and Malcolm walked to the south-west corner.

Lights were still on in the flat above the tailor's shop; the vestibule and inner doors on the side street were still unlocked. The hallway was thick with the smell of old dust and old garlic.

"And with the vital essence of Spitano, I

suppose," said Gamadge, "if they live over the shop. By the look of it they've been doing business there for half a century."

They climbed the stairs to the third floor, where fresher odours of Italian cookery met them. An old gas bracket, converted to electricity, showed them a front door with the Spitano card on it. The Spitanos were having a party; loud music came through the door, shouts and female cries of merriment.

"I don't believe he stopped off here," said Malcolm.

"Neither do I."

"I'm sure he went up to the top."

They climbed again, into darkness and a curious sense of desolation; the desolation of airless places that have been abandoned, to which nobody ever comes. Gamadge put on his torch.

There was a wall bracket, very ornate, at the head of the stairs; its bulb was dead. The skylight, immovable under its layer of dust, would let only a filtered daylight into these premises at midday. The walls had at some time been decorated by hand with a big scrolled dado in brown and gold; the pinkish plaster showed a big square place where some large picture had hung; there was a hole in the wall where its screw had been.

Gamadge said, turning his torch on all this

ancient splendour, "Done in the nineties, and the same man did the door."

It was a black door, its panels painted and gilt; but there was a Yale lock with new scratches around it.

"Mr. Garth Clayborn tried to get in?" Gamadge ruminated. "Silly fellow; the door's solid."

"They'd better be, in this place, with the outer doors open to the town," said Malcolm.

"Who'd burgle here?"

An old card under glass beside the door said *Raschner*. Gamadge put a finger on the push-bell.

"O Lord, don't do that!" begged Malcolm. "This place died long ago. What mightn't answer your ring?"

"Let 'em come."

But nothing and nobody came. The bell rang, but faintly. Gamadge turned away.

"I don't know what you think," said Malcolm, who had spent most of his adult life in France, "but I think this used to be somebody's petit apartment."

"Love nest," said Gamadge. "You may be right. At the turn of the century this would have been a good address for a sporting character; right among the big restaurants and the theatres — the hot bird and the cold bottle, the lobsters and champagne. But it's in use now. If it weren't, Garth Clayborn wouldn't have followed somebody down here at some not too remote period, and then come back, after the discovery of the Fitch murder, to refresh his memory. It looks as though he'd never got in."

"How are *we* going to get in? Shall I go somewhere and get a chisel? If the tenant is somebody up at the Clayborn house, we won't be caught here this evening."

"Let's go and talk to Mr. Spitano."

"Why on earth should he know anything, or tell us if he does?"

"He or his forebears have been living downstairs for a long time."

They went down to the floor below and rang a loud buzzer. The door was flung open, letting an uproar of voices and radio into the hall; a dark man in his shirtsleeves asked what was wanted.

"Oh, I'm sorry," said Gamadge. "You have a party."

Several children had poured into the narrow hall and were gazing at the visitors. The dark man said: "Just Sunday night."

"Too bad to bother you. It's this housing situation."

The dark man looked as though he couldn't do much for them in that line.

"It's this effort the city's making to get us

roofs over our heads," said Gamadge. "I had a list of possible addresses, and I think one of them is the top floor here. Do you know where I could apply?"

The dark man looked over his shoulder, shouted "Papa," and then turned and left without more ado: herding children in front of him and leaving the little hall-way vacant. A very old Italian, also in shirtsleeves, came through one of the doors and advanced to within ten inches of Gamadge. He looked at him, looked at Malcolm, looked at their top-coats, and put out a polite finger. He traced the line of Gamadge's shoulder seam, and asked admiringly: "Where did you get?"

"I got it so long ago I don't remember. Is this Mr. Spitano I'm talking to?"

"I am Spitano. The apartment upstairs is not for rent."

"O Lord, some mistake."

"So many people trying to find apartments, they get mixed up."

"You're quite sure the place isn't for rent, Mr. Spitano?"

"I ought to be sure; it's mine. I sublet."

"Oh, I see. You couldn't ask your tenant if he spoke to anybody about letting it?"

Mr. Spitano, who looked a little thoughtful, said nothing.

"We really thought somebody would be

there," said Gamadge. "We came on the dot, hoping to be let in to view the place."

There was another pause, and then old Mr. Spitano embarked on family annals: "When I first came to this country I took the three upper floors for the business and the family. Then my sons and daughters married, and I have only one son and his family with me now. So I sublet."

"They fixed it up, didn't they?"

"Oh, yes, a splendid place; with a beautiful painting in the hall. I put it inside; I didn't want to be responsible afterwards."

"Afterwards?"

"I sublet," said Mr. Spitano with some pride, "to Mr. G. K. Raschner."

"G. K. Raschner, Mr. Spitano?"

"Yes. The wine king. He knew my brother-in-law in Italy, and he often came to me here for little jobs of work; mending, pressing, even suits of clothes."

"But, Mr. Spitano — G. K. Raschner has been dead for years."

"Fifteen years and more," agreed Mr. Spitano. "But the flat upstairs was kept on."

"By the family? Do excuse me, Mr. Spitano, but I can't get it straight. Raschner had a town house here in New York, and an estate up the Hudson, and a villa at Cannes, and a little place on the Thames in England. Why should he need a flat too?"

"Just to stay overnight in sometimes, and give after-theatre parties. My wife kept up his apartment for him, and then my daughter, and now my grand-daughter takes care of it. But it's not much used any more."

"But — do please excuse me, Mr. Spitano — Mr. Raschner only had that second wife, that he married off Broadway."

"Yes, she was in the chorus," said Mr. Spitano.

"And she's dead too. I read about her being killed in an automobile accident in France. Who kept the place on after that?"

"Mrs. Raschner never came here," said Mr. Spitano.

Gamadge smiled. "Perhaps she didn't even know about the flat?"

"Oh, yes, she was at the parties before they were married. I thought some relative of hers kept the flat after Mr. Raschner died."

"You thought . . . ?"

Mr. Spitano hesitated. Then he said: "We didn't see Mr. Raschner often; Mr. Raschner used to leave the monthly rent in an envelope in the mailbox. If he was going abroad, he left the rent in advance; always in cash."

"Didn't write cheques?"

"No, I never saw a cheque of Mr. Raschner's. The money has always been there in the mailbox, just the same, since he died."

Gamadge studied Mr. Spitano with interest. "You mean you actually never *saw* the new tenant, Mr. Spitano?"

Mr. Spitano shrugged slightly. "Maria gets a note under the door when the flat has been used; very, very seldom now. She goes up and cleans — just a few glasses to wash, once or twice the bed made. She cleans the whole apartment twice a year, she takes care of everything — all Mr. Raschner's beautiful things. They are just as they used to be, when Mr. Raschner brought in caterers and his own butler, and gave the big suppers. I asked him not to leave silver, only plate, beautiful plate it is. But he laughed; he said burglars wouldn't come to this address, and nobody but his own friends knew he had a place here."

"And being your sublet, it was all your own business. I see."

"Good business," said Mr. Spitano. "The rents go up, go down; but that two hundred a month for the rooms and service — it has always come."

"I don't blame you for wanting to keep your tenant, Mr. Spitano."

Spitano hesitated again. Then he said: "If the tenant wants to put the flat on the market, I won't object. It's a responsibility, I won't live forever; the house might come down — they're talking about all kinds of improvements since the elevated went. What would I do with the furniture up there, the paintings and the plate?"

"What, indeed, if you can't communicate with your sublet?"

"I can't even reduce the rent," said Mr. Spitano plaintively, "and I would reduce it for a good tenant now."

"Well, I'll certainly go back to these agents and get more information; but I do wish we could see the place first, before we do anything more. Suppose we didn't feel that it would suit us? And you'd want to leave a note for the tenant, wouldn't you, in case it did suit us?"

Mr. Spitano said that the sublet hadn't been in, so far as he knew, all summer, and might not be in again for months. "I knew it was some friend of Mr. Raschner's," he said. "I was used to taking in Mr. Raschner's rent, it seemed just the same to go on taking in the sublet's rent. But it isn't so satisfactory any more. I wouldn't like my family to have any troubles if I died."

"Then you'll take us up to look at the place, Mr. Spitano? Save us an extra trip if we find it is for rent?"

Mr. Spitano turned his head and summoned an invisible person whom he addressed as Maria.

Maria was a pleasant young woman in her Sunday best. She went and got her keys, the party trooped upstairs, and Mr. Spitano pished at the lack of light. Maria went back and got another bulb.

When Mr. Spitano saw the scratches around the lock of the Raschner door he pished again.

Maria said: "They weren't here when I put up the curtains three weeks ago, Grandpa."

"Now they've found their way," said Gamadge, "let's hope they won't come often."

"We never had a burglar," said Mr. Spitano. "It's too much responsibility."

Maria said demurely that the sublet was so nice, always left her a nice present and didn't make any trouble.

"It's too long," said Mr. Spitano. "Fifteen years is too long."

Maria inserted her key and pushed open the door. The little hall-way was like the one below, but only in extent and plan; it was papered in red stamped velvet, there was a parquet flooring, and along the parquet lay a runner soft to the feet. Maria turned on a light with a red silk shade; its wall bracket was an old gilt sconce, probably Florentine. The ceiling had been painted in the Italian manner with plenty of silver and gold, and — shutting off any view of the flat beyond — a red velvet portière hung to the floor.

"Perfectly obvious," said Gamadge, "that it's a splendid place."

"Just wait," said Maria, drawing back the portière. "Just wait and see."

XIV

SWEPT AND GARNISHED

Gamadge and Malcolm walked ahead of the Spitanos into a corner room so large that Mr. Spitano had to explain it. Mr. Raschner, he said, had removed partitions.

"There is only this room and a little bedroom," he said, "and a pantry-kitchen and bath. Just right for a bachelor. *Two* bachelors."

Maria turned on red-shaded lights to display more of the cut-velvet crimson wallpaper, which was without other blemish than a few streaks of fading. Four long windows, two at the front and two at the side, were hung with long, padded, crimson-velvet curtains, each curtain decorated waist-high by a twelve-inch monogram in gold thread. The same monogram — *G.K.R.* — had been woven into the fitted crimson carpet, and was repeated on the velvet backs of the carved-oak chairs.

Everything was big and ornate, from the furniture — round dining-table, sideboard, chest, tabourets and chairs — to the plated-silver water pitcher and goblets on the buffet. Everything was a reproduction of a good antique model, and had cost money. There was a Turkish corner, a broad and low divan under a canopy. Maria turned on the perforated brass lamp under the canopy, to display the oriental splendour of the big, scratchy pillows — silk and satin, little mirror spangles, gilt braid. She plumped up an immense velvet pillow with *G.K.R.* on it in tarnished galloon.

"Magnificent," said Gamadge. "But what a lot of work for you, Maria."

"My husband helps me. Not much dirt gets in here."

Malcolm was wandering about looking at art objects — a big Buddha with an incense burner in front of him, gold-framed copies of Italian old masters; a lamp made of coloured glass, a Chinese tub on a lacquer stand, from which rose an artificial palm. "No wonder Raschner wasn't afraid of burglars," he said. "He spent a lot of money, but nobody except a theatrical supply house would have any use for any of this now."

Maria went over to a window and drew back a curtain to show off the long lace drapery beneath. "Grandma used to launder them herself," she said. "I have to send them out. They're as good as new."

"Only six dining chairs," remarked Gamadge. "Mr. Raschner's little suppers were very intimate."

"But the best caterers brought them," said Spitano. "Such terrapin, such sorbets, such champagne — Mr. Raschner always had a vintage champagne set aside for his parties. And afterwards, nothing taken away. Such good things left for the children! Cakes and bonbons, spun-sugar ice-cream nests, crackers and fancy mottoes. This tenant — no; we never have caterers on the stairs nowadays."

"It's really extraordinary, Mr. Spitano, that none of you has ever laid eyes on the tenant."

"Well, why? The sublet comes after we are all in bed — late, very late. The sublet goes next afternoon, when we are all busy."

"I see." Gamadge looked about him. "Closet space here?"

"No, none," said Maria, crossing to an arched door. "All the closets are in the bedroom or kitchen. Here is the kitchen."

"Not modern," said Mr. Spitano, "I won't say it's modern, and if ice was wanted our iceman would have to supply ice — as he did for Mr. Raschner; but ice is not wanted."

"The sublet only drinks a little whisky now and then," said Maria, "with water and no ice."

Gamadge and Malcolm looked into a clean

and tidy kitchen-pantry, with a polished copper sink. Maria showed them shelves full of curly china.

"No!" said Malcolm, backing away from a row of Bohemian glasses with blue and pink blobs on them. "No!" He shut his eyes.

"I have never broken one," said Maria. She led the party through the big room to a doorway in the south wall.

"No wall safe, I suppose," suggested Gamadge, "since you say there's no silver."

"Oh, no, there never was any wall safe."

The bedroom was almost a square, with two east windows. Once the elevated had crashed past Mr. Raschner's pillow, but perhaps Mr. Raschner had slept sound after his little parties. He had had a good bed to sleep on — wide and low, a copy of an Italian four-poster; with curtains, and a spread, of heavy silk as good as new.

It was not a large bedroom, and the bed, a chest of drawers, a night table, and two chairs pretty well filled it. Maria opened a deep closet, where hangers and shoe-rails waited.

"Mr. Raschner left beautiful robes and pyjamas here, and his slippers," said Mr. Spitano. "And a set of razors and toilet things. The sublet, no."

"I put soap in the bathroom always," said

Maria, "but the sublet brings his own."

"Ghosts don't need razors," observed Malcolm.

Maria put up a hand. Spitano laughed. "The sublet is not Mr. Raschner's ghost. We have heard footsteps."

"And found the drags of whisky." Gamadge went into the bathroom; sure enough, there was a large pink cake of scented soap on the pedestal washstand, another in the holder on the ledge of the spotless built-in tub. Mahogany encased the tub, and the interloper walked on mosaic.

"The plumbing is in good order," said Mr. Spitano. "We never had it modernized."

"It would suit me," said Malcolm. He opened the hanging cabinet, and saw empty glass shelves.

"Many a man," remarked Gamadge, "has been traced by his toothpaste; or a hair from his comb." He looked around, at the glistening walls where sea nymphs and dolphins disported themselves in swirls of foam, at the long mirror above the tub, at the glass light fixtures, up at the blue-green ceiling. "Very nice indeed."

They came back into the big room, and Mr. Spitano addressed Gamadge haltingly: "I hope you will get in touch."

"I'll try, Mr. Spitano; but I'm beginning

to think I shan't succeed. Might I say that you are probably right in wanting a change?"

"It would be better to have things regular. I am so old, and there are so many changes everywhere."

"You know, I don't believe this place was ever down in Mr. Raschner's inventories at all."

"If it had been, perhaps there would have been inquiries when his estate was settled."

"I really think so."

Mr. Spitano looked up at Gamadge anxiously. "I didn't want to lose my sublet. When the depression came, who else would ever have paid that rent?"

"Who, indeed?"

"Who would anyway, in this neighbourhood? And if I tried to rent it as a loft, there are so many new fire laws."

"I don't blame you a bit, Mr. Spitano; I don't think it was up to you to inquire. But I think you're right to want the thing regularized now." Gamadge put a bill into Maria's hand; she closed the hand tightly and smiled.

As they parted on the landing below, Mr. Spitano made one last halting observation: "I always wondered why nobody came to look over the furniture. All that fine damask linen, all monogrammed."

The two supposed victims of the housing shortage went downstairs and out on the street. Across the avenue a cab was lumbering northward; they hailed it and boarded it. Gamadge asked the driver to go up Fifth and stop at the corner below the Clayborns'.

"Less of a crowd at the alley," he explained to Malcolm.

After a pause Malcolm said: "The old man isn't a crook."

"No."

"I hope he won't get into any trouble over this."

"Why should he? Lots of landlords in New York don't know much more about sublets than he does about this one. But of course the old boy always knew he was taking a chance, dispensing with formalities."

"Pretty damn ghostly, wasn't it, that hide-out? Who *is* the sublet? Old Gavan? He's the right age to have known Raschner, but *would* he have known Raschner?"

"On the quiet he might very well have known him as a pal of the night life."

"Seward and Leeder would have been old enough to know Raschner; and after Raschner's death Seward could have stored his loot there — the mandarin robe, the emperor's seal, the tea-pot, the buttons. The Spitano woman would have dusted them and thought nothing of it; everything in the place is authentic art to the Spitanos. But . . ." Malcolm frowned.

Gamadge smiled. "But Leeder knew the sporting world?"

"It does tie up with the Sillerman thing, doesn't it? I gather from what you tell me that Raschner would have been likely to know the Sillerman girl."

"If we did research we might even find that Raschner's wife and the Sillerman girl were alumnae of the same schools of dancing."

"It's a solemn thought," said Malcolm, "that the Sillerman girl may have been at parties in Raschner's flat."

"If she was prominent in Broadway circles Raschner would certainly have known her."

"Young Garth knows who the sublet is," said Malcolm. "Will he tell us, though?"

"I'm only afraid he may tell the sublet first. I shouldn't care to be in his shoes when he breaks the news to one of those people up there — that the Sixth Avenue hang-out is discovered. I telephoned to Nordhall to watch over him."

"You did?"

"Before I sat down to supper."

"Oh. But look here — why does the sublet keep the place on? There are no rowdy parties, no parties of any kind; the Spitanos would hear them through the ceiling. There's very little drinking. Is it drugs, Gamadge?"

"Well, you saw the incense burner."

"Of course! Joss sticks would kill anything else. But there's no cache there."

"The sublet is very careful to leave nothing there."

"But Raschner left a good deal. Did he just forget about it, or did he mean to donate it to Spitano, or did he just pass the whole outfit along to his society pal without benefit of notary?"

"He died suddenly of a stroke, and the wife married again in England. She may not have known or cared what happened to the stuff at Spitano's, or the flat either; Raschner left her very rich."

"Well, it's something out of the *Arabian Nights*."

"New York's full of such mysteries; all big cities are full of them."

They had reached their corner. Gamadge paid off the cab, and he and Malcolm walked east. They passed the big apartment house, whose entrance was on the avenue, and came to the narrow entrance of the alley. Beyond it was the fence and side yard of the little old rustic house, a left-over from the time when this part of the island was rural. It was two storeys high, with a flight of wooden steps to a latticed porch, and a deep basement. It had been white, but was now oyster-coloured.

Activity boiled about it. There were two men on the roof, two policemen stood in the alley and bawled at them, and an old lady craned up at them over the porch rail. She had the look that unsheltered old ladies get in New York — alert but fatalistic.

"Tell them the fire isn't here, Officer," she was saying.

The men on the roof — one of them impeded by a camera — climbed down to the roof of the porch reluctantly. Then they began to swarm down the porch post nearest them, one after the other. The old lady retired through her fan-lighted doorway and shut the door.

The two men favoured the police officers with a stare of unutterable contempt, and walked away. One of the officers went back along the dark alley, lighting himself with his torch; the other turned to look unamiably at Gamadge and Malcolm.

"No admittance," he said.

"I thought I'd try for a short cut," said Gamadge. "Lieutenant Nordhall expects me."

"Then go around to the front, and send in your name."

"No reason on earth why you should believe

me, of course," said Gamadge. "But would you mind telling me whether Mr. Garth Clayborn came home?"

The policeman looked at him silently. After a long pause he said: "Came home a good while ago."

"Thanks."

They turned away; as they rounded the Fifth Avenue corner, Gamadge said: "We're too late."

"What do you mean?" Malcolm looked shocked.

"Didn't you see the way that officer gazed at me when I asked about Garth? Everybody but us has the news by this time."

"But, great Heavens, you telephoned to Nordhall as soon as I told you —"

"Garth simply drove down to the next block when you lost him, turned east, and came back up here. He may have been here several minutes before you called me from that drugstore. The officers had no reason to report on him, and there are back stairs. Nordhall and Mulvane were on the ground floor, and the Nagles and Elena — and Leeder, if he hadn't left — were in the dining-room. They'd been there ages, though; but I have a kind of feeling that they'd stay there as long as they were let alone. From Nordhall's account I gather that there was a tremendous spread, and I can't see Nagle hurrying away from his drinks and his supper. Elena was going to stand by, I think. But Nordhall will have all that by this time."

Malcolm said: "I don't know why you're so sure that something's happened to the poor idiot."

"I've had him on my mind; all I needed was that policeman's look when I mentioned Garth's name."

They turned the Clayborn corner. There were more cars in front of the house, a sort of van waited at the kerb, and a milling crowd besieged the vestibule. They shoved their way through and as far as the front door. The officer guarding it took their names.

"Who's this with you?" he asked Gamadge.

"My assistant."

They were passed in. Elena Clayborn dashed forward to meet them, and cast herself into Malcolm's arms.

"David," she gasped, "Garth's dead."

XV

FLORAL BELLES

Malcolm received the onslaught with aplomb. He patted Elena affectionately on the head and said he knew, and that it was too bad.

"But, David, what shall we do? It isn't like a murder that happened a long time ago. I feel as if I were going crazy. It happened right here, right upstairs, while the Nagles and I were in the dining-room."

"And Mr. Leeder?" Malcolm was looking at Gamadge above Elena's topknot.

"Roly'd gone off again somewhere. He's sitting in there with the Nagles now in the library, and he won't say a word; I never saw him like this. They're all different. Uncle Gavan is wandering around all bent over like an old man. Aunt Cynthia is in her room crying. Crying! I didn't know she could. Father's in an awful state; he's lying down, and he won't let me in."

"You ought to get out of here."

"But I can't leave them."

Nordhall was coming down the stairs.

Recognizing Malcolm and catching his eye, he jerked his head in the direction of the reception-room; Malcolm nodded, stood Elena gently on her feet, and put an arm round her shoulders. He urged her along the hall and through the arched door.

When they had gone, Nordhall came the rest of the way down the flight and stood for a moment looking at Gamadge. Then he said: "I didn't lose a minute."

"Neither did I."

"He got here before you telephoned me, contacted his party, and was shot dead. Shot twice. Know why nobody heard the gun?"

"Why?"

"Because the shots were fired in a sound-proof room that I didn't lock behind me."

"Oh."

"Come on up."

They mounted two flights of stairs through a silent house. On the top landing Nordhall paused to dismiss a young policeman whom he addressed as Matty, and then stopped in front of the closed music-room door.

"What did you find out?" he asked.

Gamadge told the story. Nordhall listened, nodded once or twice, asked a question or two, and then reflected, chewing on his lower lip.

When he finally spoke it was in the conversational tone of one who abandons surprise: "By the time I got to the dining-room — that was while you were taking Malcolm's call — Garth was already in the house. We get that from the men out back; he came in in a hurry. I went into the dining-room and settled to a meal; the Nagles and Elena Clayborn were there, Leeder had left. Leeder says he had a sandwich and a drink, and then went up to talk things over with his ex-wife; but she wasn't having any — she'd gone to her room. He didn't like to knock, afraid of disturbing her; so he went and sat in the sitting-room and thought things over by himself. You can't see the stairs from where he says he was.

"I took my time in the dining-room, had supper and coffee and went over my report — such as it was. It was as good as a play, listening to the Nagle girl putting on airs to Elena Clayborn; telling her about the big shots her father knew, and how she would do modelling if she didn't think office work was more realistic, and how girls all ought to do something. Elena Clayborn didn't say anything, just listened to her blow. It seems Elena Clayborn does hospital work morning, noon and night.

"The old folks were sitting down to their supper, no stand-up buffet for them; tucking in a big meal, and Nagle trying to pass wisecracks with old Roberts — who brushed him off like a fly. Nagle was putting away plenty of Scotch, probably thinking of how much Gavan Clayborn was going to come across with.

"Mulvane put his head in and said I was wanted on the telephone; that was you. I rounded up Sergeant Crowley and young Matty, and we went through the house. But would you believe it, we looked in there" — he jerked his head — "last of all. Logical in a way. The door was shut, the wire from the hall had been detached and slung inside. The men thought I'd locked the place before I left. I was hunting around for the boy downstairs; when I came up here and saw the closed door, I went for it naturally. But I didn't even then think I was looking for a dead body.

"I always knew there was a kind of wild character somewhere in the house, but I didn't know how wild until I saw Garth Clayborn lying in there. Shot twice. Do you know what with?"

As Gamadge made no reply, Nordhall told him: "Shot with the gun that killed Sillerman. How do you like that?"

"Astounding."

"Isn't it?"

"How do you know?"

225

"Well, we haven't got the gun."

"No?"

"And that's funny, too, isn't it? But it's natural enough for the boy to have agreed to talk to his prospect in the music room — the one place they absolutely knew they wouldn't be overheard or interrupted. But the prospect was heeled. Well, they sent me the Sillerman files and the Sillerman bullet, and the bullets that killed Garth Clayborn came out of the same old Smith & Wesson .38." Nordhall jerked his head again, this time in the direction of the closed studio. "We've got a regular laboratory set up in there, everything that wasn't nailed down at headquarters. Easier to bring stuff here than to take five people downtown to have their hands examined for powder traces. Not a trace on anybody, and no stained gloves in the house."

Nordhall unlocked and opened the music-room door; he switched on his torch. The silvery place was as it had been, except for two dark stains on the rug midway between door and window.

"Both the bullets went right through," said Nordhall, "head and chest. You can imagine the mess, and it must have sounded like two bombs in here. Would you mind telling me why Garth Clayborn let anybody walk in on him wearing gloves? Or let the prospect

226

put on gloves while they were talking?"

"I might make a guess."

"Go ahead."

"The prospect might have had some story about being allowed by the police to take a breather in the garden. Why not? There are police out there. It's a cold night, it would be natural enough to put on a top-coat and gloves — no hat, though. The revolver would be in a side pocket of the coat, wrapped in cleansing tissue."

"That's an idea."

"Easy enough to dispose of shredded gloves."

"Down a drain?"

"I wouldn't risk a drain; things get caught in traps."

"Not in these traps," said Nordhall.

"They might. The murderer remembered that there's a stiff breeze. What could have been simpler than to cut the gloves into shreds, open a window, and let them go? They'd be half over the city in five minutes."

"The pistol wouldn't blow away, but unless it was dropped out and somebody picked it up and walked off with it, I don't know where it can be. We've had men on the roof, and on the roof below the bricked window there — a gun could have been poked out of the hole we broke through. I'd say it isn't in the house. Of course we're right near the Park, plenty of tough characters along there of a night; perhaps it was thrown out from the roof to the street and picked up. Whatever became of it, it was fired as soon as the killer got inside the room and got the door closed. Garth Clayborn stood about the middle of the rug, as you see, facing the door."

"I see." Gamadge asked after a moment: "How much of a search have you made for the gun? You wouldn't give up yet, would you?"

"We'll give up next Christmas. We've about settled for the chimneys and flues, we've had every book out of every shelf, we've done the usual tearing up. We can't locate a secret panel, and the whole family says there isn't one. We won't take their word for it. Now I suppose you'd like to see the Sillerman files."

"That's in order."

"You bet."

They went out and along to the studio. Nordhall opened the door, and Gamadge looked in on a scene lighted by the concentrated glare of one hooded lamp. It shone on a long work-table set out with apparatus, and on the hands of the expert who sat, eyes shaded, looking at something which he held in the delicate grip of a forceps.

Nordhall said: "Mr. Gamadge, Norris."

Norris looked up. He said: "Glad to meet you."

"Ready to go to court, if we ever get there?"

"Yes; but I'd like to get the gun. It would be fine if I could fire a bullet out of that gun."

"We'll get it for you if it's in the house."

"How about the roof?"

"You stick to your microspectroscope. The gun isn't on the roof."

"I suppose those cameramen were trying for a picture of you people searching the roof," said Gamadge.

"What cameramen?"

"The ones on the poor old lady's roof down on the next street."

"We've been all over her place outside; the party might have slung the gun there."

"I wish you'd tell her it isn't a fire; she'll sit up all night on account of sparks."

"Keep your mind on the nice tie-up here," said Nordhall, who was looking through papers in a folder. "We'll have you busting a twenty-year-old alibi for us before we're done with you. I'm surprised at you, not finding us that pistol."

"You've cramped your style," said Gamadge, "with that nonsense about its being thrown out of a window. Just make up your mind that it's in the house, and then of course you'll find it. Nothing makes a thing harder to find than a preconceived idea that it may not be findable."

Norris said: "You're right at that."

"Oh, yes?" Nordhall was irritated. "You tell it to the boys down in the cellar with coal dust in their hair."

"They're fondly dreaming of the underworld character who happened to pick it up on the street," Gamadge told him.

"Well, what are *you* dreaming of, then?"

"I'm dreaming of Sir Arthur Wilson Cribb, Lady Athenia Lewis, Dante's *Divine Comedy, III*, and what other of the lot may be —"

Nordhall, with a howl of rage, dashed from the studio.

Norris looked up mildly, detached and faintly interested.

"They make boxes out of books, in this house." Gamadge picked up the folder, went across the studio to a chair beside a lamp, turned on the lamp, and sat down.

"Don't say." The scientist fitted one of his bullets into a little labelled case. Silence reigned until Nordhall returned panting. He held in both hands, by its edges, a thick quarto in black morocco gilt.

"Doggone you, Gamadge," he puffed, "you can find anything in a book." He slapped the volume down in front of Norris. *"Floral Belles,"* he recited loudly, *"Of the Greenhouse and Garden. Profusely Illustrated With Coloured Plates From Paintings by Mrs. A. Walton,* 1873. Heavy as lead anyway, I suppose Matty just took it out of the bookcase and laid it on the floor." He raised the heavily stamped and gilded cover, and displayed the big revolver that lay in a roughly-contrived nest, wadded with tissue. "The cover was glued down."

Even Norris deigned to bend forward and peer at this exhibit. "Smith & Wesson .38," he said admiringly. "What do you know?"

"They have this pink tissue stocked in all the bathrooms here," said Nordhall. "Go to it, Norris. I won't touch it. You have two witnesses and not another thing on your mind."

Norris picked up a heavier pair of forceps, gently drew the gun from its nest, and placed it gently on a rack.

Nordhall peered into *Floral Belles.* "This is no job like those others we saw," he said. "This is a strictly amateur performance, imitating the others in a clumsy way. This was done in a hurry, to hide that pistol. Wonder why our friend kept it after the Sillerman murder, though?"

"Not a type to discard a weapon," said Gamadge.

"Probably been in this book twenty years

until to-day. Fresh wadding, though. Don't these people read their books?"

"Not old gift books of the vintage of seventy-three," said Gamadge. "It was quite a safe bet."

"Dug out with a jack-knife, and not too sharp a knife either. Pages not even glued, and here are some left in underneath, and a picture. Boy oh boy, look at the Night-blooming Cereus. Size of your head. Will you fingerprint, Norris, and right away?"

"I'll try."

"Don't blame you for thinking there won't be any." Nordhall straightened himself. "It's going to be tough for us. Inference, with that old phoney alibi to keep getting in our way."

Gamadge was reading typed pages with deep interest. He said: "This list was typed verbatim from Sillerman's address book, was it?"

"Yes. You can see the original if you like." Nordhall added with a grin: "In confidence. That's confidential matter, as you may judge."

"O Lord, I feel as if I were handling a dud bomb."

"Some list, isn't it?"

"Some list. Did you get after all these unfortunates?"

"Only to find out whether they were in town on the night. None of 'em was except our friend, so far as we could trace names."

"*Massinger*, and a Chicago address. Was that one of the L. L. Massingers, by any hideous chance?"

"It certainly was, the old man."

"Well, he's dead."

"Guess he wished he was when we called him up. Of course he didn't have to say why he was in Sillerman's book — only had to give us his alibi. Same with the others."

"And this Pittsburgh party; *Considine*. Sillerman was discreet, it might have been old Considine or his sons."

"It was the youngest son, and he was married, like Leeder."

"Philadelphia, Washington, even Atlanta. Whew. What a circle of acquaintance. I suppose you never followed up to see whether there was any later drug history in any of these cases?"

"Why should we, and where would we get the money and the time?"

"*Leeder*," read Gamadge. "And this very same address, and here we are, digging up the past."

"Makes you think, doesn't it?"

"Oh, fate caught up with him long ago, when the janitor saw him. Otherwise —"

"Otherwise he wouldn't have had to kill Fitch for her savings, and steal things out of the house. Well, we can take him downtown. But I wish we had something more, anything, just something to take it out of the probability class and put it where it belongs. As it is — but you know what a trial for murder is. This gun connects him with another murder that he had an alibi for."

Norris leaned back and lighted a cigarette. He said: "This gun is polished off clean. What's the chance of your getting after those Leeder alibis now?"

"One's dead. One's in Europe doing army stuff — big shot. One's married and lives in Canada. But we can ask them questions, of course, the live ones," said Nordhall, with ferocious gaiety.

Gamadge was studying his list. He said: "Here's a name with a star after it and no address. *Colford.*"

"You'll find three or four of those; nothing could ever be done about those."

"Did *she* star them?"

"Yes."

Gamadge knitted his brows over Colford.

"They're all names like that," said Nordhall. "Tilson, Albury, made-up sounding names."

"Might be drug merchants. She'd have to be extra careful about those."

"They widened the field," said Nordhall.

Elena dumped silver into a felt-lined basket, while Roberts watched her nervously. The forks and spoons had probably acquired more scratches in that moment than in all the years of their long lives. Malcolm, his chin on top of a pile of Crown Derby, stopped to say between his teeth: "They care who shot him."

"Why should Ena care? Her father is out — he isn't the type at all; that's all she has to worry about, and it isn't much. You've led such a sheltered life, Ena, you don't realize how often these things happen. They happen all the time. Whoever did it will get a verdict of temporary insanity, and after that it'll be one, two, three."

"Years?" asked Gamadge.

"Just a little rest cure in a sanatorium. Whoever it was probably found Garth rooting around in that music room, still looking for buttons or something, thought he'd discovered the person that killed Aunt Aggie Fitch, and had a brainstorm and shot him."

"With the big gun the person always carried around in his pocket," said Elena. "You ought to have studied law. You're good."

"That's why they'll say it was insanity — because the person carried a gun."

"I wouldn't call it insanity to carry a gun in this house," muttered Malcolm. He disappeared through the swing door into the pantry.

"They'll never find out who did it," continued Miss Nagle. "They can't even *find* the gun. We'll all get a certain amount of publicity, which never hurt anybody yet, and then it will all be over. Now what I suggest is that you come home tonight with me. We're all out of it — Dad and Mom and I and you. I say stay out of it. You can share my room, I'm away working all day anyhow. Rowe Leeder will be there — you like him."

Malcolm, who had returned from the pantry and was unpinning his dish towel, gazed at her as at a fabulous monster. Two tears welled up in Elena's eyes; Roberts put out an old hand and patted her on the arm.

Gamadge said: "Your parents went some time ago, Miss Nagle; you elected to stay?"

"Ena had to have somebody her own age — somebody in the family."

"Most kind of you indeed. As a matter of fact, Miss Clayborn's father has asked me to give her a message — he wants her to go elsewhere tonight."

Elena stared. "Wants me to go?"

"Yes, but hotels are pretty hard to get into at a minute's notice nowadays — any notice; and it's late to arrange a visit with friends. I suggested your spending the night at my house. I called my wife, and she's delighted to have you."

"Magnificent idea," said Malcolm, looking puzzled.

"Malcolm will take you," continued Gamadge, "and he and you can see Miss Nagle on her way home."

Miss Nagle said: "Why shouldn't Ena come home with me?"

"Because you are a member of the family, as you yourself remind us; and you and your father and mother will have to deal with a certain amount of that publicity you spoke of. You don't object to it, but Miss Clayborn does. With us she'll be out of circulation."

Elena said: "I can't just run off like that. It would be brutal."

"Your father asks it as a favour to him. He wants you out of the house tonight, Miss Clayborn."

"I'll go up and speak to him."

"He's had one of those sedatives he takes." Gamadge held out a sheet of note paper. "Here's his message."

Elena took it and read it. Then, silently, she handed it to Malcolm. It contained three pencilled, sprawling words: *Elena, Please go.*

"Mandatory," said Malcolm.

"Yes, I'll pack my bag."

"Why wait for that? Why bother?" asked

Gamadge. "My wife can supply you with what you need for tonight, and there are drugstores and toothbrushes on your way."

"If I'm going, I'd *rather* just go," said Elena. "I can't bear to go upstairs. If it weren't for Father, I couldn't bear the house."

"Have you a coat down here?"

"Yes."

"Then put it on and — er — fly."

Elena went through the swing door. Presently she returned in a tweed top-coat, with Miss Nagle's coat over her arm. Miss Nagle silently put the garment on, took gloves out of one of its pockets and adjusted them, looked up at Gamadge and made a dry remark: "Quite the hustler."

"You'll find the back way clear," said Gamadge.

They went out by the kitchen lobby and back door; a policeman was waiting for them with his torch, and the two young women descended into the garden. Malcolm, with a final questioning look at Gamadge, followed them.

Gamadge came back into the kitchen. He said: "You must be more than ready for bed, Roberts."

"The young people did most of my work for me, Sir."

"I'll help you with the last of it. The usual tray."

"Do they want the tray tonight, Mr. Gamadge?"

"More than ever. I'll carry the heavy stuff — the bottle of whisky and the siphon."

"Thank you, Sir."

They went into the dining-room, where Roberts got out the big silver tray and placed glasses on it. He counted them with a frown.

"Mr. Clayborn and Miss Clayborn," said Gamadge, "Mr. Seward Clayborn, Mrs. Leeder, Mr. Leeder, and myself."

"Mr. Seward Clayborn, Sir?"

"He didn't want his daughter upstairs again, Roberts. Too hard on her, all this. She would have tried to see all those distraught people — too hard on her."

"Yes, Sir."

He ranged the six cut-glass highball glasses on the tray, got out the silver ice bowl and tongs, opened the lower cupboard of the sideboard. He stood looking in at the array of bottles.

Gamadge said: "A wonderful and beautiful sight."

"Yes, Sir. I was just thinking. The others — they all take Scotch, and they all take a good stiff drink. Mr. Garth — he would never touch anything but rye, straight rye, with a little water afterwards. I knew him from a baby: he wasn't a troublesome boy. It was just that he hadn't anybody of his own here; he used to be with us servants too much. He was a good-natured boy, Mr. Gamadge."

"Must have been a bad shock for you, Roberts. You've stood by nobly."

"I never thought I'd be glad to retire until to-day, Sir."

"I hope they'll take good care of you."

"They will, Sir. And I have my annuity coming in from the trust."

"That's good."

Roberts got out the Scotch, and then went back into the pantry with the ice bowl; when he returned it was full of cubes, and he had the siphon in his other hand.

Gamadge took the whisky bottle and the siphon, Roberts took the tray, and they went out into the hall and up the front stairs.

When they reached the sitting-room, Roberts put the tray down and got the folded coffee table from a corner. He extended the two leaves, placed it in front of Mrs. Leeder's seat before the fire, and put a log on the embers. Gamadge added his load to the tray, and then carried it over to the table.

"And now, Roberts," he said, "you're to quit."

"Yes, Sir; but I must put out the lights, Sir."

"I'll do that."

"The dining-room, Sir?"

"All of them. Forget it."

"Thank you, Sir."

Gamadge followed the old man into the hall, followed him through into the back passage, and watched him mount the back stairs. Then he came into the hall again and closed the passage door. Nordhall had just come down from the top floor; he addressed Gamadge gravely: "I've seen them all except Mrs. Leeder."

"What luck?"

"All right, I think, but I'm having a little trouble with Seward. I've got to go back up to him. Will you speak to Mrs. Leeder? I think she'd take it better from you."

"I'll speak to her."

"That's her door at the end, on the left."

Nordhall went upstairs again. Gamadge walked to the east end of the hall, and knocked on the left-hand door.

After a moment Mrs. Leeder's voice came faintly to him: "Who is it?"

"Gamadge. I'm sorry to disturb you."

"Come in."

Gamadge went into the room, asked: "May I close the door?" and at her nod closed it. He said: "We must talk a little, Mrs. Leeder; I shouldn't like to run the risk of being overheard."

She was sitting on a chaise longue between

the front windows, and she had been looking out into the dark. She did not move except to turn her face towards him. "Who would listen?" she asked.

"You mean the listener is dead?"

"Why was he killed, that wretched boy?"

Gamadge brought up a chair to face her. He sat down and glanced about the room. It had been bright and luxurious once, with its bamboo furniture and its draperies of blue satin, its cheval glass, its flowered rug; but blue fades, and the satin had been replaced on the chaise longue and the chairs with cretonne which was now fading too.

"Why was Garth killed?" she asked again, her pale lips hardly moving.

"He'd found out a secret. There's a flat downtown that somebody now in this house went to and paid rent for."

"A flat?"

"It belonged to a man named Raschner, who died years ago. Garth must have followed somebody down to it at some time, and this evening he went again. He never got in, but I did. It's obviously a hide-away. Deals for art objects could have been made there, drugs taken there. The boy probably came back here and told somebody that he had information to give away — or sell."

"You mean he was blackmailing someone?"

"There must have been good reason for killing him; it was a risk."

"I should think it would be easy enough to find out who rents this flat."

"Even the landlord doesn't know."

"How did you find it?"

"I remembered what you told me about Garth's ways, and when he went out this evening I had him followed. He must have thought that the place would tie up in some way with the Fitch murder."

"Does it?"

"There's a sort of connection. Raschner may have known the Sillerman woman."

"The Sillerman woman! What connection —"

"When there are two murders traced to the same set of people, the police don't as a rule expect to find two murderers, only one; and the two murders twenty years ago were committed only a couple of weeks apart."

"The Sillerman murder was never traced to any set of people."

"They've traced it to this house now."

She sat up to stare at him.

"They've found the gun."

"The gun? The gun that killed Garth?"

"It killed the Sillerman woman too."

She gasped: "I can't believe it."

"It's a fact, Mrs. Leeder. It was in a book

— *Floral Belles.*"

"That old funny flower book?"

"Somebody got the idea from your solanders, and hacked out pages to make a hiding place. The gun has been here ever since the Sillerman murder, and it was used again tonight."

She raised her left hand, in which her handkerchief was tightly clenched, and pressed the back of it to her forehead. Gamadge caught a faint wave of delicate perfume. She said: "I wish my head didn't ache so. I can hardly think. But I can see that it's part of the old plot."

"Leeder didn't put the gun there?"

"Of course not. The whole thing has been engineered by someone in this house; everything's been done to incriminate him, and I couldn't do anything until now." She stood up, tall in her velvet robe. "Where's that man Nordhall?"

"He's rounding up the family, or trying to. He wants to talk to them all before he takes Leeder downtown."

"He won't take him downtown. Will Rowe be there too?"

"Yes."

"Where?"

"In the sitting-room. I lent a hand with the whisky tray, so it will all seem quite the normal evening session. People are easier when things go on as usual." He added: "Elena won't be there."

She turned her head to look at him.

"I sent her off with Malcolm," he told her.

"Where?"

"To my place for the night."

"Thank you for that." She stood moving her head from side to side like a blind thing hunting for light; then she walked down the room to her dressing-table, dropped the wadded handkerchief on it, and got a fresh one from the drawer. She tinkled glass, and when she turned Gamadge caught a wave of fresh perfume. He asked: "Are you up to it?"

"Quite."

They went out into the hall. Norris stood near the stairs, looking what he was — the skilled professional, with nothing of the policeman about him. He nodded politely when Gamadge introduced him to Mrs. Leeder, and then addressed Gamadge with a hint of dry amusement:

"The Commissioner came."

"Oh bother."

"Nordhall has him upstairs, you can imagine the talk. I'm to get the people into the sitting-room and stand by."

"That's good. Have you a gun, by any chance, or do you just use them for purposes of comparison?"

"I can use a gun. Nordhall lent me his."

Mrs. Leeder said: "I don't know why Mr. Norris should need a gun."

"Somebody might not like what you say. All right, Norris," said Gamadge. "You'll find us waiting for you. All just as usual."

"All just as usual," agreed Mrs. Leeder in a muffled voice.

Norris went upstairs, and Gamadge and Mrs. Leeder went into the sitting-room. She walked directly across to her place behind the tray, and sat down. "I'm glad you helped Roberts with this," she said. "Glad for more than one reason."

Gamadge settled himself on the sofa opposite her. He said: "I'm quite sure you'd be the better for a drink. I know I should."

XVII

ACTION

Mrs. Leeder was herself again, or nearly so. Once again she lifted her clenched hand to her forehead, as if there were a pain behind it which might be reached by pressure of the perfumed handkerchief; then, as if realizing that the gesture was nervous and automatic, she let the hand fall to the tray. After that, except for the slight working of her fingers at the folds of the handkerchief, a jerky, tearing motion, she was quiet and calm.

She picked up the silver ice-tongs, and looked at Gamadge. "How do you like it?"

"Any way."

"The family likes them good and strong." She put ice into two glasses, poured whisky, filled the glasses from the siphon, handed Gamadge his drink across the tray.

They both drank. Gamadge said: "A very present help."

"Isn't it?"

"Hadn't it occurred to you, until I spoke to Norris about the gun, that you might be in danger yourself?"

"It wasn't until you told me about finding the gun in that book that I was a danger to anyone."

"And now you know you can be?"

"Yes," she said sombrely, her eyes on the dark gold of the liquid in her glass. "Now I know I can be. But things don't seem quite real to me yet — it's as though I had been deafened by a bomb." She looked up at him. "I suppose it was you who told those policemen where to find the pistol?"

"They would have found it themselves; I thought of it first, that's all."

"They never would have found it. Admit that they never would have."

"Well — perhaps not."

"Do you know what I wished, when you told me?"

"That you'd never asked me to come to this house?"

"Yes," she said dryly. "And then I realized that if you hadn't found the pistol in that book, I never should have remembered."

"Remembered what, Mrs. Leeder?"

"I won't say anything until I can say it to the person's face."

Their eyes met. He said: "You're too scrupulous."

"Can one be?"

"I thought yesterday that you were too brave. I was actually a little afraid that you mightn't be available when I came back this afternoon."

"How melodramatic."

"More so than the facts?"

Gavan Clayborn came slowly in, walking as if he had come to the end of a long journey. He did not look at Gamadge or his niece, but sank into his accustomed chair and frowningly busied himself with cutting and lighting a cigar. Mrs. Leeder dropped ice into a tumbler, her face expressionless.

Miss Clayborn came in with short, tottering steps. She had changed into a negligé, a dark-blue velvet robe bordered with rose, and her hair was bound with a rose-coloured plait of ribbon. Her eyes were blank until they saw the whisky tray; then they took on an avid look. She came and sat at the near end of Gamadge's sofa. Mrs. Leeder put ice into a tumbler.

Seward Clayborn came in, looking a very sick man; yellowish, drawn, with dull eyes. He wore a dark dressing-gown over pyjamas. He was passing behind the sofa to his favourite window, but Mrs. Leeder asked: "Don't you want your drink, Seward? Wait a minute."

He paused, staring away from her at nothing. She put ice in a third tumbler, poured whisky, filled all the glasses. Gavan picked up a glass to hand it to his sister. Mrs. Leeder asked sharply: "What's the matter, Seward?"

Everybody turned to stare at him. He was standing as he had stood before, gazing vacantly at the picture over the mantel. When she spoke he started, said: "Nothing," in a low voice, and then, after a moment, took the glass she offered him. He went over to the window, turned his back on the room, and with one knee on the cushioned seat, one hand clutching the edge of the curtain, looked out at the street.

Leeder came in, with Officer Crowley beside him. He stood within the doorway surveying the scene, until Mrs. Leeder poured a drink and held out the glass. He said "Thanks, Harriet," came forward, and took it. Turning with a smile, he said: "All right, Buddy, I'm coming back." He returned to Crowley's side. Norris appeared in the doorway.

Gamadge leaned over, reached across Miss Clayborn to pick up the Cribb solander from the table, opened it, and handed it to her. She took out a cigarette with fumbling fingers. Gamadge offered it to Mrs. Leeder, who shook her head. He turned to look at Seward over his shoulder, held out the box, and asked: "A cigarette, Mr. Clayborn?"

Seward started violently. He steadied himself by catching the window curtain, cleared his throat, and said huskily: "Thanks. No."

Mrs. Leeder's eyes were on him. She said: "Well, here we all are, and there are two policemen to take care of us. Perhaps it will be safe for me to ask you whether you've all heard about that flat that Garth discovered downtown. Mr. Gamadge has just told me about it."

Nobody answered her, or seemed to breathe.

"And he has just told me," she went on in a clear, cold voice, "that they found the gun that killed Garth in a book downstairs. One of Grandmother's books, I remember it well; a book about flowers. I didn't make it into a box; I wonder who did?"

Pale faces stared at her; all but Seward's — his was turned away.

"And Mr. Gamadge says," she went on, "that that gun they found in it is the gun that killed the Sillerman woman all that long time ago."

Leeder said, or rather shouted: "What do you mean?"

She smiled at him. "You didn't know, did you, Roly? It was here all the time. Now do you understand what's been happening to you all these years?"

"My God, I don't understand anything."

"No, why should you? But you will. We all ought to drink to your health; the man who always takes the blame."

Seward, as if in obedience to the suggestion, raised his glass to his lips. She laughed.

"Seward needs that drink," she said. "He knows what I mean. I can tell you who put that gun in the book in the library." And then, as the figure in the window swayed, clutched at the curtains, and suddenly pitched to the floor, she screamed: "What has he done? What has he done?"

All the others were on their feet, Norris had already reached the side of the fallen man. He said sharply to Leeder, who had pulled away from Crowley's restraining hand and was now bending over the window seat: "Don't touch that glass." Seward's highball tumbler lay tilted on the cushion, its contents dribbling into the velvet.

Gavan stood rooted, his sister had sunk down again on the sofa and covered her face with her hands. Norris, on his knees beside the figure that rolled on the carpet, was shouting orders to Crowley: "Get them here with the ambulance. He isn't dead."

Mrs. Leeder said in a frozen voice as Gamadge swung back to face her: "He's taken the best way out. Why do they try to save him?"

"You have definite evidence against him?"

"Of course I have. I came into the library once when he thought we were all out; I saw him looking at that old flower book. I mean he was just putting it away."

Leeder came around the corner of the sofa and stood in front of her, looking down at her. He said: "Harriet, for God's sake: *Seward?*"

"Why do you think he poisoned himself, Rowe? Anybody could see the state he was in before — ever since he came into the room."

It was the sudden change in his face, as he looked past her, that made her turn and glance up over her left shoulder. Nordhall had come around the edge of the screen, between it and the fireplace. He moved fast, leaned over the back of the sofa to grasp her left wrist, and with his other hand took the crumpled handkerchief from her fingers.

"All right, Mrs. Leeder," he said. "I saw you drop the stuff out of this into Seward's highball, after you had everybody looking at him and away from you. Even Gamadge had to look away, but he knew what you were up to, and he knew I was on the job and watching through a crack in the screen. He gave Seward the signal, and Seward only pretended to drink. He didn't let all the whisky out of the glass, either — plenty left to analyse."

She sat for a moment like a woman of stone, then slowly turned her head and watched while Seward got unsteadily to his feet. Crowley had an arm about him, and Norris was lifting the highball glass from the window seat.

Nordhall carefully worked the handkerchief open with the fingers of one hand, and peered into it. "Plenty of crystals here, and you had to use plenty of perfume to cover up the smell. Gamadge was sure you'd grab a chance to clamp the murders on somebody, and so we gave you one. Seward was our best bet, but we warned all the others except Leeder; Crowley would have spilled his whisky for him if he'd started to drink it. This is bad stuff to fool with. Gamadge was sure you'd have something ready for yourself in case something went wrong."

She sat like an archaic statue, her hands flat in her lap with the fingers pressed together; her features had a primitive look, expressionless, blank and dead.

"But even if you hadn't had your chance now," continued Nordhall, "you'd have taken it later. Somebody in this house would have got poisoned, and that would have satisfied Leeder. That's all you were afraid of — Leeder."

His grasp on her left wrist had loosened,

now that he had the handkerchief away from her; and the fingers of that hand, still pressed together, rose like lightning to her mouth. Even then he would have been too quick for her, but Leeder lunged against him, across the sofa, with the whole weight of his body. The impact threw Nordhall off balance for a moment, and in that moment her fingers had reached her lips. Leeder, sprawled half on top of her, had her in his arms when she collapsed.

Crowley dragged him to his feet; he did not resist, but stood trembling as Nordhall raised the woman. Norris came over and stood watching. After a moment he said: "Don't think it's any use, Nordhall."

"Get the ambulance anyway," snarled Nordhall. "They sometimes live."

Gamadge said: "She didn't have any dinner."

"That does it," said Norris. "Hydrocyanic on an empty stomach — no cure for that."

Gamadge looked at Leeder. He said in a low voice: "You managed it for her, anyhow."

"All I could do," said Leeder. "All I could do."

Miss Clayborn, her face hidden, sobbed aloud. Gavan came up to Leeder and put a hand on his arm. He said: "Wish I could say something. Wouldn't do now. But we'll stand by you."

XVIII

UNKNOWN QUANTITY

Gamadge sat relaxed in a deep armchair drawn up to the office fire, Malcolm sat relaxed in another. The little table between them held whisky, and they had each had a long drink.

"I wouldn't have been in your shoes," said Malcolm, "when you drank that highball she made you."

"I had to drink it; I was watching that left hand of hers with the handkerchief in it, watching pretty sharply; but she wasn't going to poison *me*."

"Why did you think she was likely to have poison on her?"

"People like Mrs. Leeder always keep an out for themselves, and I knew she'd be jittery after Garth's murder; she hadn't planned for it, she had to work fast. She couldn't be absolutely sure that she hadn't left any traces. There were none, of course — she was so clever."

"Nothing tangible," said Malcolm, with a smile.

"I couldn't help noticing, of course," added Gamadge, "that she kept that handkerchief rolled up in her left hand."

"Will they have the heart to do anything to Leeder for obstructing justice?"

"I don't think they'll do a thing to him. They ought to call it a conditioned reflex; he'd been protecting her for twenty years, of course he went on doing it. He didn't love her any more, but that didn't come into it."

"And knowing he didn't love her any more, she wasn't sure he would go on protecting her — with the evidence of the gun against her and somebody else likely to go to jail?"

"That was why she had to have another suspect — so that Leeder would allow somebody else to go to jail. She didn't dare let *him* go; he might not be obliging enough to die for her. She hoped to persuade him that Seward was guilty. Extraordinary thing," said Gamadge, "that nobody ever seemed to realize there were two people named Leeder in the Clayborn family when Sillerman was killed."

"They all assumed it was Leeder because he'd been seen by the janitor."

"That was what convinced me he wasn't one of Sillerman's clients, and therefore wasn't a regular visitor — because he was seen by the janitor. If he knew the ways of the establishment he wouldn't have been seen. He would have known when it was safe to call."

"I suppose Mrs. Leeder was being black-mailed by Sillerman, and had to tell him about it?"

"Or had to get money from old Mrs. Clayborn, who consulted Leeder."

"What was she being blackmailed about, I wonder?"

For an answer, Gamadge took an envelope out of his pocket and emptied it on the table. Hard crumbs of a resin-like substance lay there, and Malcolm peered at them.

"That," said Gamadge, "is the real thing. None of your home-grown product. That's hashish from India — it's to be bought still, or was before the war, in ports of the Eastern seaboard. Nordhall found it, and more, lying about quite openly among her cosmetics; who but a professional, who'd been on the Narcotics Squad, would be likely to recognize it? She got more than one idea from Sir Arthur Wilson Cribb."

"She didn't impress me as a drug addict. Did she keep the Raschner flat to take this?" Malcolm fingered some of it.

"I don't think she can ever have been a drug addict in the usual sense of the word; this was something in the nature of an experiment at first, I suppose, a new sensation; then something to have recourse to on occasion when life became too dull. Of late years — certainly this last year, according to Spitano, who had no reason to lie about it — she wasn't resorting to the splendid place more than once in six months."

"Did she originally take over the Raschner flat simply to take this, I wonder?"

"I doubt it. Perhaps she missed the Raschner parties. She must have known Raschner well, when she was a wild girl in a wild era — that era Theodore likes to tell about — before she was married. If she was blackmailed by the Sillerman woman after she was married, and Leeder went down to settle, and couldn't settle, and afterwards the Sillerman woman was shot — well, what could he do? Inform the police that he had no evidence, but that the murderer was probably his wife? Poor old Mrs. Clayborn must have known the facts; she doesn't seem to have had her stroke the moment after she had talked to Leeder, but she left him his legacy. She might have helped him over those first thin years, but she died. Mrs. Leeder pretended to be suffering from a broken heart on his account, but I don't think there was any pretence about her being against the divorce. As her husband, he couldn't have been called as a witness against her if suspicion ever pointed her way."

"Why did he come back? To watch her?"

"Miss Clayborn tells me she found out where he was working, and got him to come back. As Gavan intimated, she was very fond of him; and I rather think," said Gamadge, smiling, "that Miss Clayborn's sort would be inclined to tolerance in the matter of homicide when the victim was a Sillerman and the culprit a Leeder. But Leeder, of course, had terrible reasons for keeping an eye on his ex-wife; he was the only living soul who knew what she might be capable of. She must have been horribly afraid of him. When the Fitch murder broke he'd suspect her first of all; he suspected her of another, he knew what her life had been, and he knew that she had always been hard up. He'd believe at once that she had stolen the buttons and the Pekin loot and sold them."

"So she had to think up a defence that would satisfy him."

"She had twenty years to think one up, and when she finally decided on one it was brilliant. A striking illustration," said Gamadge, pushing the bits of hashish about the table thoughtfully, "a striking and ironic instance of the limitations of a warped and brilliant mind. The egocentric brain wishes to use other people's brains, and can't realize that in every intellect there's a personal variation from the norm — call it the unknown quantity. She called me in to use my intelligence, probably because her attention had been drawn to me by you. I suited her purposes admirably, or so she thought; but if I hadn't been at hand she would have managed with somebody else whose special knowledge in the matter of books wasn't as convenient as mine, but whose intelligence she would have helped along. Allsop, perhaps."

"What was this defence of hers?"

"Take it from the beginning. Of course she must have read the Cribb journals before they were made into a cigarette box; and to have used them afterwards as she did she must have had a strong conviction that nobody else in the house had ever read them. Some years later she applied the method of strangling used by the Assassins of India, fully described by Cribb, when she killed Aggie Fitch. No reason for her to destroy the solander on that account; to destroy it would be to call attention to it, and nobody would ever connect it with the Fitch murder or with her.

"But it was always about the house, it was often under her eye. At some time she conceived the idea of using it to exonerate herself, while fixing guilt on someone else in the family.

"Not Leeder — anybody but Leeder. It was for Leeder's benefit that the scheme was to be contrived. She fixed on Seward, for obvious reasons. He would be a logical suspect, in any case, to the police. He had taught her to make the solanders, he might well have read the Cribb journals before he converted them, he had contacts with art dealers and connoisseurs, some of whom might be unscrupulous — I'm afraid the tribe has that reputation — when it came to getting unique objects of art at a bargain. And Seward was a nervous invalid; mightn't he be taking stronger drugs than those prescribed for his headaches?

"Well, she had decided to use the solander by calling my attention to it, and then by hiding it in the library. Nordhall followed the lead like a lamb, and made all the proper deductions: if she had let me see it, if she had discussed Thuggee with me — or rather had let me think of Thuggee — she had no guilty associations with the solander or with Thuggee, and it wouldn't have done her any good to hide it afterwards. For Nordhall she was out.

"And she didn't undeceive him at the time. I had no more than the faintest wisp of theory then, I had nothing remotely approaching evidence against her until I saw the Sillerman files. When I saw them I immediately told Nordhall what my theory was, and we immediately put it to the test."

"But I don't know why you didn't agree with Nordhall — that the murderer had hidden it after your unexpected visit on Saturday, hoping you hadn't noticed it."

"There was an alternative to that theory, an alternative which removed a faint suggestion of coincidence — the bane of logic."

"If you accepted the whole thing at its face value there was no coincidence. Why didn't you?"

"There was no coincidence," agreed Gamadge, "except in the fact that when I sat at tea in the sitting-room yesterday, Sir Arthur Cribb was at my elbow."

"But that was where it had always belonged — in the sitting-room. I've seen it there myself."

"Where?"

"On a table just across from the fireplace, beside a big lamp, where people sit and smoke." Malcolm suddenly stared.

"And not," said Gamadge, "on a little crowded table at my elbow, where Mrs. Leeder could call my attention to it naturally, simply, and without calling attention to her own insistence. When Garth Clayborn came in, you know, he seemed to look for it on that table across the room.

"It was just possible that my attention had deliberately been called to the subject of

Thuggee, with a victim of something very like Thuggee lying dead upstairs, to be discovered the following day. And I was to be present at the discovery.

"And coincidence can only be explained away by purpose. Whose purpose? Only Mrs. Leeder's, since only Mrs. Leeder knew that I was to be there on Saturday. And Mrs. Leeder had heard of me, she knew my interests, she could hope that I would know the Cribb journals and that I might see them among the other books in the library. She might not have to help me along at all, and that would be so much the better for her.

"I did see the solander among books in the library; and while Nordhall followed the deductions that Mrs. Leeder had laid out for him, I told myself that it might indeed exonerate Mrs. Leeder; but that it might on the other hand *be* there to exonerate her.

"If it was, then she was guilty of the Fitch murder. If it was, then everything obscure about the case took on coherence — the Sillerman murder, Mrs. Clayborn's failure to deprive Leeder of his legacy, his return, and his curious attitude towards Mrs. Leeder. My mind, in fact, didn't work as she had every reason to expect it to.

"And it betrayed her again later, when I guessed that the Sillerman gun was in *Floral*

Belles. She thought it never would be found."

"It wouldn't have been, if you hadn't thought of its being in another of those book boxes."

"She had introduced me to them. She had reminded me what handy and deceptive receptacles they can be, so when the gun wasn't to be found I naturally thought of another solander. It gave her a hideous shock when I told her the gun was found; she knew nothing about bullet markings, and thought the gun by itself would betray her to Leeder. That brilliant and resourceful mind — it worked fast. I told her the whisky tray was in the sitting-room as usual, and she saw her great chance and seized it — she could pour the drinks herself. She'd have tried some other way, of course, if the whisky tray hadn't been there; put the stuff in Seward's bedside water-jug, or in his medicine; I don't know. But when I mentioned the tray, she went straight to her dressing-table and got the poison ready in her handkerchief."

"Kept the other dose for herself if things went wrong?"

"Yes, under flesh-coloured courtplaster, on the inner side of the first finger of her left hand. Nordhall doesn't blame me for letting myself be out-guessed about it. He was out-guessed himself."

"She did out-guess you?" Gamadge looked at him, and he said: "If she hadn't, would you have tipped Nordhall off?"

"That's the kind of question no man is obliged to answer."

"I mean I wouldn't have tipped him off. But I've known her longer than you have — the whole thing is a staggering shock to me."

"My own part at the last was odious, but I can't say I feel remorse. She'd killed three people and was ready to kill another, she'd exploited Leeder in a way that can only be described as savage, and she was the coldest hypocrite I ever saw or heard of. Of course the long wait for the discovery of Fitch's body had dehumanized her; Garth drove her into action again, and by the time the gun was found she was on the edge of madness."

"I don't know how you ever got the Clayborns to go through it tonight."

"Nordhall and I had to explain what we thought she was trying to do to Seward; even then, it wasn't easy to persuade them to play the game. They were terrified of the poison — I was, at the last; there was a moment when only Nordhall could see what she was doing with it — and I think they were afraid she'd manage to get it into somebody somehow, no matter how careful they were. But she'd martyrized them in the matter of the loot from Pekin, and Seward's life was in danger from her, and she'd never given any of them much reason to love her. We shall probably never know the full details of their life with her in that house. Uneasy, I feel sure."

"I suppose Leeder could fill in a lot of gaps," said Malcolm, after another interval for reflection.

"He never will. Tonight, of course, he couldn't be asked anything; he was practically out on his feet. The Commissioner really did come later, and a couple of other bigwigs that knew Gavan, and Gavan had the family doctor in. Among them they settled it that Leeder could stay there until he got his wits back. There's nothing the Clayborns won't do for him; they know a gentleman when they see one. They always thought he killed the Sillerman woman; they didn't know a thing about Mrs. Leeder's connection with her. Nobody did except Leeder — after old Mrs. Clayborn died." Gamadge rose. "Time for you to go home, time for me to get to bed. Where have they put Ena?"

"Where do you suppose? On a trestle in the laboratory? There was only one place for her, the chesterfield in the library."

"Oh, the devil. Has she been told she's got to get up early? I need my library myself after breakfast."

"I'm coming for her at half-past eight. She'll have to be told what happened — tough for her."

"Not so very," objected Gamadge. "She liked Leeder a good deal better than she liked Mrs. Leeder, and now she'll have him. And if she is able to get you up at any such hour in the morning as the hour you imply, she seems to have got you too."

"Oh, yes," said Malcolm calmly. "She's got me."

"Good."

"And I have a ghastly kind of suspicion that the Nagle girl's got both of us for life."

"Better and better. Just what you need. A little roughage in your diet and more acidity. Ena ought to be nice to the Nagles; they stood by Leeder. To tell you the truth, I rather liked them."

"You like a lot of funny people."

"Don't I?"

Malcolm, in the doorway, stopped and turned. "You didn't have to remind Mrs. Leeder that she needn't look behind the screen tonight, did you?"

"Because Garth was dead?"

"Yes. She wouldn't forget that Garth was dead."

"But if it had really been an obsession she would have looked behind the screen just the same — or started to. When she didn't, I knew that it hadn't been an obsession; it was just a part of the build-up."

"You don't think he hid there as a small boy?"

"I'm pretty sure he did. But he hadn't got on her nerves to the extent of making her still look for him behind the screen when he was grown up and out for the afternoon. She was building herself up as a victim, and the build-up was a success. That touch about the screen almost broke my heart."

"I suppose when Garth handed Nordhall that stuff about Leeder, and all the rest of it, he was throwing a smoke screen over his blackmail victim?"

"Yes. She had to be kept safe for him. Nobody but Roberts will mourn him, I'm afraid. Good-night."

XIX

A WORD OR TWO

Leeder did in fact speak to Gamadge about the Sillerman case, but not until the summer of 1945, when they met again for the first time. It was in the Malcolms' apartment, where they had been invited for supper. The Malcolms had been married for three months. Malcolm was still in the Navy, and his wife and Clara, Gamadge's wife, were in the kitchen preparing supper for four. Gamadge and Leeder had been requested to stay out of it and finish the cocktails.

Leeder was much as he had been, except that his thin grey flannels and his bench-made shoes were new. He said: "Ena thought I mightn't want to meet you. As it happens, I'm glad of a word or two."

"That's gratifying to me, Mr. Leeder."

Leeder poured out the last of the cocktails into the glasses. He said without introduction: "That Raschner gang was her finish. Not that I want to cast Raschner as the villain of the piece; he was just an old sport that liked 'em younger and younger the older he got, and thought all the little girls were able to look out for themselves and were on the make anyhow. I don't know how Harriet came to go to his parties, but she was always looking for trouble in those days, and at last she found it. Raschner's weren't dope parties, he didn't know a thing about Sillerman's side line. And I don't know what arrangement Harriet can have made about keeping his flat on. I was out of the picture long before he was dead.

"She met Sillerman at the parties, and got into debt with her for various things, including the hashish. That was before we were married. I knew she was rather wild, but so was I. We meant to have a high old time."

Leeder drained his glass, put it down, and went on:

"Harriet never told me anything about the blackmail, when it started. She knew I didn't have anything like the kind of money to meet the bill. She went to her grandmother, who did have the money, and said the claim was for old bridge debts. Mrs. Clayborn would understand bridge debts, she played all games for stakes and wasn't stiff about such things. But she didn't like the amount owed, and made Harriet say who it was for. She didn't like the Sillerman set-up. She spoke to me;

gave me the money, and asked me to go down and look into the whole thing.

"I went, as everybody knows; but first I inquired around about this woman. I got a lot of nods and winks, and I was worried. There had been certain things I didn't understand, though I never would have said Harriet took drugs, and in fact I don't think she ever did regularly. I saw Sillerman, who stuck to it that the money was for cards. She wouldn't show me Harriet's I.O.U.s, wouldn't deal with me at all.

"By the way she talked, and by the look of her, I knew it was serious. I guessed dope. When I went back and talked to Harriet she was furious with the woman — never thought it was going to be a real shakedown. Wouldn't tell me anything. I had to go back to poor old Mrs. Clayborn — nobody else in the family knew a thing about it — and say nothing doing. Did she want to hold out on Sillerman and risk a showdown or stuff in the scandal sheets? Should we risk a private detective or the police?"

"Tough," said Gamadge.

Leeder took a light from him for his cigarette. "Tough," he said. "I explained to Mrs. Clayborn that the police had special ways of dealing with blackmail, protected the victim, didn't let names come out. But what good would that do if one of those little papers they were printing at that time got hold of Harriet's name? And we didn't know what the poor girl had got into exactly, and what the damage would be.

"Twenty-four hours later, before we had made up our minds, Sillerman was dead. Harriet swore to me that she knew nothing about it, and I certainly didn't know that she owned a Smith & Wesson .38. Wonder where she bought it.

"The news broke, my name came out. When we found that there was nothing on Harriet in the Sillerman books, nothing but the surname — well; I don't blame poor old Mrs. Clayborn for being glad of that. There wasn't a thing either of us could do about me; she wanted to go to the police with some story about my going down to see Sillerman for *her* — some errand she was going to think up. Something about music, my God. The police and the district attorney and the papers would have made hash of the poor old thing. I said for Heaven's sake keep the Clayborn side out of it — I had my alibi.

"I wonder her stroke didn't come then and there. You can imagine the state of things in the house. Harriet's father and mother wild at me, naturally, and Harriet in a nervous collapse. I left without seeing her; she didn't want to see me, she had her head in the sand."

Leeder smoked in silence. Then he said: "She knew I wouldn't give her away; but when Aggie Fitch was found, and I saw that she was going to shove the murder on somebody else . . . couldn't imagine at first what she was up to, calling you in about those buttons . . ."

His voice died. Then he said quietly: "I was up against something. She didn't seem to want me to take the rap this time, she seemed to think she really had something on Seward. I was completely stumped. I had plenty of her this time, but . . . Then she gave herself away. That's why I wanted this word with you."

As Gamadge looked inquiring, Leeder added: "You settled it."

"Settled it? Fixed the guilt on her, you mean? It was a ghastly trick, but I could think of no other."

"I didn't mean that," said Leeder. "I don't blame you, somebody had to do that, since I couldn't. I mean you let her go. Let her die."

"*I* did?"

"It was the only way out for her," said Leeder, "and you let her take it. You were looking at her hands — so was I. Do you think I suppose you missed anything I didn't? It was easy enough for me to block Nordhall off, but you could have warned him first. I thought I'd just say I appreciated it."

"Well," said Gamadge, "thanks."

Two cheerful voices came through from the kitchen, telling them that everything was ready, come and get it. But as they rose, Leeder said a word more:

"I used to go up there to the top storey and stand and look at that pottery figure. I used to see through that wall. I used to dream about what was inside."

Gamadge said: "So did she."

The employees of THORNDIKE PRESS hope you have enjoyed this Large Print book. All our Large Print titles are designed for easy reading, and all our books are made to last. Other Thorndike Large Print books are available at your library, through selected bookstores, or directly from us. For more information about current and upcoming titles, please call or mail your name and address to:

THORNDIKE PRESS
PO Box 159
Thorndike, Maine 04986
800/223-6121
207/948-2962